THE LUMBERING GIANTS OF WINDY PINES

MO NETZ

CLARION BOOKS

An Imprint of HarperCollins*Publishers*

Clarion Books is an imprint of HarperCollins Publishers.

The Lumbering Giants of Windy Pines
Copyright © 2024 by Mo Netz

www.harpercollinschildrens.com

Library of Congress Control Number: 2023937116
ISBN 978-0-06-326653-7

Typography by Julia Tyler
24 25 26 27 28 LBC 5 4 3 2 1

First Edition

For all the disabled kids who never
got to be part of the adventure.
You are now.

ONE

THE LATE AFTERNOON SKY IS JUST STARTING TO TURN PINK AND bruised at the edges, which means prime check-in time. The past year of shuttling from one motel to the next has taught me that. But when we pull in under the Slumbering Giant's flickering neon sign, Mama's old red station wagon is the only car in the lot.

The *S* on the sign keeps going in and out. Sometimes it looks like it says LUMBERING GIANT instead. I picture a massive, grunting creature stomping through the trees of the North Georgia mountains and smile to myself.

"Stay here," Mama says. I watch her walk through a glass office door with a Vacancy sign hanging crookedly inside.

The last motel was turquoise stucco with a swampy pool. This one is pink brick with a sad little courtyard where someone has planted a single struggling palm tree. Next to the tree is a cracked cement cherub that looks like it belongs in a graveyard.

Unlike the last motel, this one has a second floor, with rickety-looking steps leading up to an outdoor catwalk connecting the rooms. We won't be staying up there. For obvious reasons, we always get a downstairs room.

Mama comes back smiling, followed by a woman wearing a flowered nightgown over sneakers. She's older, with pale white skin and long gray hair that looks almost blue. Dangling from a chain around her neck is a pair of those glasses that turn up at the corners. *Cat's eyes.*

"Jerry, this is Miss Mavis," Mama says. "This is her motel."

I'm surprised to see a lady manager. Most of the places have grumpy men with worn-out faces who just ask if I'll be quiet.

Miss Mavis scrunches her nose. "Jerry?" I can tell she's trying to tell from my shaggy hair and my dad's old flannel shirt whether I'm a boy or a girl. I kind of like letting people guess, at least until Mama gets out my wheelchair.

Two summers ago, I became clumsy. Well, *clumsier.* I've always been accident-prone and I'd never consider myself a star athlete or anything, but suddenly I kept getting hurt. My legs became weak and shaky; sometimes they'd just give out under me, and I'd collapse into a puddle on the floor. Then it was doctors and tests and the verdict of a genetic disorder that I'd always had but never known about, and the news that it was only going to get worse.

When it got bad enough that I couldn't walk more than a few steps without falling, a church donated the chair to us. I hate the Barbie-pink frame, but Mama's always reminding me that we're lucky they gave it to us because it's a really nice one, built to fit someone who must have been similar to me in size and shape, though it must have belonged to a very different kind of girl than me. (Also, it wasn't even our church and technically we're Jewish.)

Mama wheels the chair around and pops open my door. I grab the top edge and steady myself to stand up, then sit back down in the seat. Miss Mavis looks at the frame and nods like she's decided something. She's putting me in the "girl" box in her head now for sure.

That's why I hate the pink. Not because I have anything against the color. I just don't like people making up their minds about me so easily.

"Yes, this is my daughter, Jerusha," Mama says, turning toward me with a *now play nice* expression.

I nod.

"Well, I don't expect *you'll* be any trouble," Miss Mavis says, bending at the waist to put her face at my level. That makes up *my* mind about what kind of manager *she'll* be: there are the ones who think I'm going to be loud and break things (even though I'm almost twelve), and the ones who expect me to be a juvenile delinquent because I'm not in school. Miss Mavis is the type who sees my chair and thinks I must be an angel. It's not the compliment she thinks it is.

Straightening her back, she hands a key on a clunky plastic ring to Mama. Miss Mavis's hand looks papery next to Mama's, which is the same white-but-not-pale color as mine that people call *olive* even though that sounds like it should be green. Mama jingles our room key in the air. "C'mon, kiddo. Let's go check out our new home."

She turns quickly so her hair, as dark as mine but gathered into a long ponytail, swings out wildly behind her. I follow, gripping my handrims and pushing my wheels as fast as I can.

The room smells like stale cigarettes and dust. Mama lays our suitcases across one of the two not-quite-full-sized beds and pops open the latches.

"We're going to be here long enough to put clothes in the drawers?" I ask.

"This is it," she says. "This time we're staying."

I roll myself up to the side of the bed and open my case. I'm not sure how much I believe we're not going to bounce to another motel when the season ends or the work dries up. It's been that way ever since my dad died last year and we lost our house. We stay in the small towns, keep to the back roads where you can find places like this that are cheap and have rooms without stairs. We haven't been able to find any affordable apartments that don't have them. Motels at least have doors that are flat to the ground, and since the rooms have to be wide enough for housekeepers to pull carts of laundry through, they're also wide enough for my chair.

I tried going to the schools in the towns, but the last one was so awful I said I was never going back. I'm officially homeschooled now, which just means I read a lot of books.

Books are, for the most part, what's in my suitcase. I have a few novels, some history books, a dictionary, and Encyclopedia Britannica volumes *B, E, G, P,* and *R.* They're packed under a thin layer of clothes that used to be my dad's. His flannel shirts still smell like him no matter how many times we wash them. I wrap myself up in them and it feels like he's hugging me.

"I have it all planned out," Mama says. "I got work right here in the motel. Steady work, so we can really settle in."

"Okay," I say.

She sets a hand on my shoulder, the hand wearing both her wedding ring and my dad's. His ring is too big and slides around on her finger. We're both trying to fill in his space.

"Listen," she says. "I know it seems like we've just been floating from place to place, but I've been trying to get us here for a while now. I want us to stay put. I want that for you, okay?"

"Okay," I repeat, but this time I try harder to mean it. It's not like staying in one place means all that much when you don't have friends, but I know she's trying. So I decide I'll try, too.

"I have to talk to Miss Mavis," she says. "You'll be okay here?"

"Sure," I say. After she closes the door, I turn on the AC and the TV and fill the room with the hum of motel sounds that are always the same. There's something comforting about that.

TWO

ONCE MAMA'S GONE, I TRANSFER ONTO THE EDGE OF ONE OF THE beds. As I shift my weight, I can feel Paul in my shirt pocket, curled up tight. He's good at staying out of sight when people are around.

Now that it's just us, he crawls onto my shoulder. Unfolding his wings, shimmery like pigeon feathers, he shakes himself out and stretches to his full length of about six inches from his snout to the tip of his tail.

I know I invented Paul in my head piece by piece. The pigeon-colored wings came from actual pigeons that perched on the window ledge of a place that was in a small city. We stayed on the fifth floor, where you could see most of the city out the window, and the first thing you always saw was a pigeon. The manager of that place hated them. *Rats with wings*, he said. But I thought they were beautiful.

"It's dark in there," Paul complains into my ear. "I don't see the point of all this hiding when nobody can see me but you."

"Because it's annoying when you breathe down my neck while I'm concentrating," I tell him.

Paul is a dragon, though a fairly useless one due to his size and the fact that he doesn't breathe fire and can't fly. He can flap his wings and sort of hover for a few seconds, but he doesn't go anywhere. He blames me for this. He thinks since I'm the one who imagined him, I could have made him fly. He also thinks I could have given him a movie-star voice instead of a nasal grumbling that sounds like my great-uncle Hershel (and a cooler dragon name than Paul).

It doesn't work that way, though. When you don't have any friends, your mind sometimes makes one up for you. But I didn't choose any of the things that make Paul who he is. Instead, I woke up with a tiny dragon friend made up of pieces of my memories.

Here in room 118 of the Slumbering Giant, Paul the Fairly Useless Dragon makes himself at home by shimmying up one of the pillows and reclining with his arms (Do dragons have arms? His front legs?) propped behind his head. "Relax," he says. He pats the pillow next to him.

I wiggle my head around on the pillow and stare up at the ceiling. The walls are wood-paneled, but the ceiling is made of that crumbly-looking white material that looks like cottage cheese, like a piece of it might just crumble off and land on your head while you're sleeping.

A crackly hiss floats from just beyond my elbow. I turn to the end table, where the clock radio has apparently turned itself on. I switch it off, but the static keeps flowing out of the speakers, wrapped around distorted voices saying words I can't understand.

"What the . . ." I mutter, thumping my hand hard against the side of the radio. Finally, it shuts off. "Piece of junk."

"So," Paul says. "If we're staying, whaddaya thinkin'? You gonna go back to school?"

"No way," I say.

The last time I went to school, maybe six months ago, we were staying in a Wild West–themed motel on the edge of a little farm town. I'd dealt with bullies before, even before I got the chair. Kids who made fun of my funny walk or my secondhand clothes or the way Mama cut my hair around an actual salad bowl. But the kids in that town were *mean*, throwing paper wads at me in class and empty soda bottles at me as I wheeled across the parking lot. Once a kid sitting behind me tried to set my hair on fire. The last straw came when Corinne, the meanest of the mean girls, pushed my chair down the steps with me in it.

There were only two steps. The arm I landed on turned out to just be sprained, not broken, and the footrest on my chair that got twisted out of shape was eventually hammered back into place. The worst part was the way everybody gathered around but nobody helped. They all just laughed. Corinne said it was an accident.

School was just me and my books after that.

"Why did she do that?" Paul asks. He's been watching my face; he knows I was thinking about Corinne.

"She thought I was only pretending to need my chair," I said. "She saw me stand to reach something off a shelf, and she said if I really needed a wheelchair, I wouldn't be able to move my legs."

"That's silly," Paul says. "Your chair is just a tool. Anybody can need one, for a lot of different reasons."

"But some people don't get that."

Paul shakes his head.

"Anyway, I found out she told some other kids she was gonna prove I could walk. That if she pushed my chair down the steps, I'd stand up."

"But you didn't."

"I couldn't. I didn't know she was behind me until it was too late, and then I just . . . *fell*." I shudder, remembering the feeling of the ground dropping away under my wheels.

The door opens, and Mama walks in with her brows scrunched together. "Jerusha Eliana Blum, were you talking to yourself again?"

I shake my head. "Just watching TV."

Mama presses her lips into a tight line. She's talked to

me about Paul before. A grief counselor at some support group told her he was a coping mechanism to deal with my dad's death, and that in a few months I wouldn't need him anymore. But he's still here, and whenever Mama catches me talking to him, she makes that face.

I don't want her to start in about dragging me to a counselor as soon as we can afford it, so I try to distract her by making space for her to sit down next to me. To my relief, she does, just inches away from Paul, but of course she can't see him. I shoot him a look anyway, and he scurries off the pillow and back into my pocket.

"You need to spend time with kids your own age," she says.

"Kids my age are overrated," I tell her.

"*Kids your age* don't usually have imaginary friends," she says. I know the difference between fantasy and reality, but I swear, my pocket doesn't *feel* empty. "And they don't usually read dictionaries for fun."

"I learn a lot of new words that way. Like *chimera*. Do you know what *chimera* means?"

"Stop trying to change the subject."

I roll onto my side, pulling the pillow with me. "I know you're worried," I say. "But I'm fine. I promise." Her face softens a bit, so I change the subject for real. "Tell me about your new job," I say.

She gives in. "I'll mostly just be cleaning the rooms,

doing some small repairs here and there, but you can stay here during the day, and I can check in on you."

"I don't need you to check in on me."

"*Or* you can call if you need me, and I'll be close by," she says pointedly. "Miss Mavis has some other stuff she'll be having me do for her that might take me away for a night or two. But I'll still be close."

That perks up my interest. "What kind of stuff?"

She pats the mattress next to me and stands up. "I'll tell you more when I know more."

LATER, AS WE LIE IN BED WITH THE LIGHTS OFF AND THE HEAVY curtains drawn, I listen to the wind whipping through the trees. It sounds like singing. Or crying. This town is called Windy Pines, and it doesn't take a genius to figure out why.

"Mama?" I whisper.

"Mm?"

"Tell me again about the golem."

I hear her blankets rustle as she turns to face me. "A golem," she says, "is a creature. Usually a giant. Made of clay or mud or dirt, that becomes alive, but not really human. But they can help humans."

"Like the one that helped Uncle Hershel and Aunt Ruth."

"Your uncle *claims*," Mama says, with a hint of laughter in her voice, "that they built a golem with mud from the banks of the Vistula River, and it carried them here, across the ocean from Poland. As the waters grew deeper, its legs grew longer, always able to touch bottom."

"I like that story."

"I know you do," she says. "You get that from the Blum side of the family." My dad's side. "Except," she says, "you don't even need mud to make your creatures. You just create things with your mind."

I glance over to where Paul the Fairly Useless Dragon is sleeping—and snoring—curled up on the pillow beside me.

"An animal that's a combination of parts of other animals," she says.

"What?"

"That's what *chimera* means. Either that, or an illusion that's impossible to achieve."

I can sense her smile in the darkness. "I can read the dictionary, too," she says. "Now go to sleep. It's late."

THREE

WHEN I WAKE UP THE NEXT MORNING, MAMA'S BED IS ALREADY made and she's dressed, not in a housecleaning uniform but in jeans and boots. She's leaning into the mirror to pin her name tag on straight. She smiles into the glass, but it reflects back on me. "Morning, sunshine."

"Morning," I grumble as she puts in the fake-ruby earrings I made her at camp.

"I'm about to start my rounds," says Mama. "So if you need me, call." She nods at an old avocado-green landline phone. I'm *still* not allowed to have my own cell phone.

"Why don't you have to wear a uniform here? You always have to wear a housekeeping uniform."

"They're ordering one for me," she says, her gaze still glued to the phone. Then she shakes her head and drops a kiss on the top of my hair. "You'll be okay. This arrangement is gonna work out great for us. Read some books; don't just watch TV, okay?"

"I won't," I say. She's speaking code, reminding me of how I said I was watching TV when I was really talking to Paul. That's what she wants me to do less of.

"And you don't have to stay inside all day," Mama adds. "Get out and explore a little! Just . . . stay out of the woods. It's dangerous with the logging, and I don't want you in there alone."

"Okay." I've heard enough about logging accidents—dropped tree limbs, wayward logs, falls from platforms—to know I don't want to be anywhere near one when it happens.

Mama hesitates before she opens the door. "I want to talk about you trying school again," she says. "Once we're settled in."

I shake my head hard. "I can learn everything I need to in here."

She sighs, her hand still resting on the doorknob. "It might be different now that we're living in one place. You'll have a chance to make real friends."

"Mama, nobody wanted to be my friend at any other school. Why would they want to here?"

"I don't like the thought of you alone in this room all day. It's lonely."

"It's lonely being around a bunch of people who don't like you. Only worse, because they're mean. If I'm gonna be lonely either way, I'd rather be lonely alone."

"I'm sorry," she says, and it sounds like she genuinely is. Not just sorry she asked me, but sorry that it happened. "Just try going outside, at least. I think there are other kids staying here. It couldn't hurt to say hello."

When the door closes, I scoot to the edge of the bed and transfer into my chair, then roll to the bathroom. I change into clothes, then roll outside in search of the vending machine.

The parking lot is mostly empty. There are just a few beat-up cars and a couple of logging trucks. All the room shades are drawn, and the lot is quiet except for the howling of the wind and the hoot of a distant owl.

Around the corner from an ice machine that doesn't look like it's been used in years is the snack machine. I buy a packaged muffin that doesn't taste at all like blueberries but does manage to calm the growling in my stomach.

On my way back to the room, I notice lines on the pavement. It looks like they were made with colored chalk, like someone drew hopscotch squares that were mostly washed away.

Sometimes the motels we move into have other kids. But I never bother trying to make friends with them. Even if they didn't think I was a freak, either they'd be gone soon, or we would.

As I roll around the scrubby palm tree, a gleam in the dirt catches my eye. It's a small plaque at the stone angel's feet, too covered in dust to make out the words. I spit into my palm, then swipe my hand across the surface to reveal: IN MEMORY OF MILLIE DOBBS. 1923–1933. Whoever Millie Dobbs was, she was younger than me when she died. I shiver. It makes the courtyard feel even more grave-like.

The edge of the parking lot bleeds into logging roads, the blacktop giving way to dirt that forks into the woods, but there are no other buildings in sight. The forest looks like it gets dark and deep fast. Thick clouds of fog cling to the high branches of the trees, even though it's hot and clear up here in the mountains. I listen to the *OOOoooooOOooo* sound of the wind blowing. Beyond the trees, mountains arch into the smoky sky like the spines of sleeping monsters.

Before I can turn away, a red glow catches my eye, almost like an ember in a dying fire. It's gone so fast I wonder if I imagined it, until I see a shadow that I swear is *moving*.

I shudder and shake my head, then roll back toward our room as fast as I can. I'm a few doors away when I hear a voice behind me. "Jerry."

I jump in my seat. With all the howling around us, it sounds like the wind whispered my name.

Gripping my armrests, I turn around. Mama is standing behind me, her hair falling loose from her ponytail and her clothes streaked with red mud. "What are you doing out here?"

I swivel my chair toward her, rolling my eyes while I'm at it. Why can't she make up her mind about whether she wants me to stay in the room? "Exploring. Like you *told* me to."

"Right." Mama is brushing at the mud on her jeans when I turn to face her, but all that does is grind it in more. "Well, uh, just be safe. And don't go too close to the woods."

"I'm not." The woods kind of creep me out. Not that I'd say that out loud. "Why are you so dirty? I thought you were cleaning rooms."

"Miss Mavis wanted me to . . . clean out a storm drain." She points vaguely toward the edge of the parking lot that slopes down into the woods. "Over there."

"Why are you acting weird?" I wrinkle my nose.

"Why are you asking so many questions?" There's a note of laughter in her voice, and she sounds like Mama again. "See you in a bit?"

"Sure."

I wait until she knocks and enters a room, then roll to the edge of the lot in the direction she pointed. Where the asphalt ends, there's a lot of red mud leading into the woods and it's studded with footprints. Some look like the tracks of rabbits and deer and bears. Others I don't recognize—they're almost birdlike. And there are human boot prints.

But no storm drain.

PAUL IS WAITING FOR ME WHEN I GET BACK TO OUR ROOM. "Where were you?"

"I got food and had a look around."

"And you didn't think I might want to come?" he huffs.

"I needed to look by myself this time. I'll take you later."

I turn on the TV just to have some background noise. There's a newscaster on, a lady announcer with that kind of curled hair that's sprayed completely stiff. A smaller picture above her head shows a scruffy-bearded man wearing a flannel shirt.

"Another logger went missing last Friday in a wooded area outside Windy Pines," the stiff-haired lady is saying. It's that word that gets my attention: *another*. How often do people go missing in these woods? "Viewers are asked to call with any information that could lead to the location of Edwin Martinez." A phone number scrolls across the bottom of the screen.

For some reason that I don't completely understand, I grab a pen and write down the number. I guess if we're going to spend the foreseeable future living around woods that disappear people, I want to be prepared.

That's when a shimmer of static threads down the screen, cutting the newscaster's face in half. When the tweedy ribbon of interference is smack across the middle of the screen, I hear what sounds like voices. Not the lady's voice, but something deep and gruff and unintelligible. The static flips down again and disappears, leaving behind a greenish cast.

Then there's a loud thud outside, hard enough that the wall shakes. I peer through the curtains and see a pair of skinny brown legs and feet in plastic jelly sandals swing down from above and hit the metal staircase.

Two more sets of swings and thuds, and I see the girl the shoes belong to. She's probably close to my age, and her legs are dotted with Band-Aids, the fancy kind with designs on them. Her head is covered with dozens of tiny braids with rows of beads on the ends that swing and clack against each other.

When she's still two or three steps from the bottom, she grabs the staircase's rusty handrails, swings up again, and launches into the air, landing gracefully on the concrete. She lifts her arms like an Olympic gymnast, then runs over to the hopscotch squares.

"Are you gonna talk to her?" Paul asks.

I shake my head. "Why?" I look down at my wheels and

then back up at Paul. "It's not like I could play hopscotch."

"She might not care about that."

"Maybe not. But I have things to do."

Paul hops onto the page of my open encyclopedia. "Like what? Reading about"—he skitters across the page—"eminent domain?"

I sigh and slam the book shut. "I just don't see the point. People don't *stay* in places like this for long. Even if she likes me, wheelchair and all, and we become friends, she'll leave eventually."

"We all leave eventually." Paul gestures around the room in a way that lets me know he's talking about more than just the motel.

I get it. We leave homes, we leave schools, we leave Earth. Sooner or later. But when *home* is a place where most people stay for only a night, it's different.

"That's easy for you to say. You're, like, an ancient immortal creature. Everything seems temporary to you. But this—" I gesture around the room. "I mean, this room. This motel. This is not a place where people stay very long."

"You're staying a long time. I heard your mother say so."

"If we are—and I'll believe it when I see it—we're the exception." I put the encyclopedia back in the drawer and slide it closed. Then, before he can protest, I close the curtains, too.

But almost as soon as I do, I hear a car start outside the window. I tip back the curtain and see Mama driving out of the lot. Her brake lights flash on and then she turns, close enough that I can see the tail end of the car. She's turning into the woods.

The very same woods she just told *me* to stay out of.

FOUR

"SHMENDRICK," PAUL SAYS AS THE ROOM DOOR SLAMS BEHIND me. "Didn't your ma say to leave those meshuggah woods alone?"

"If they're so dangerous, why's *she* going there?" I ask, furiously pushing myself into the parking lot. "Something's up."

"There's a lot parents don't tell you," Paul says, flitting back and forth across my handlebars. "That's called being parents."

"Not Mama," I say softly. "Not me."

I think about when Daddy was dying. How, after his accident, when he was still alive but things didn't look good, Mama sat me down and told me everything. She let me visit Daddy in the hospital and read dragon books to him while the machines beeped in the background. I was sad and scared but I knew what was happening. Mama *trusted* me to know what was happening. Why wouldn't she trust me now?

I push the thought out of my head and keep rolling. "It doesn't make sense," I tell Paul as we coast down the hill. "First she doesn't wear the same uniform as the other housekeepers. Now she goes sneaking off into the woods? Something's not right. When I asked her why her clothes were muddy she said she was cleaning the storm drain over at the edge of the parking lot."

"So?" Paul says.

"So, there *is* no storm drain at the edge of the lot."

We're near the mouth of the woods, right about where Mama's taillights turned off, when I pull back on my rims and skid to a stop. The trees fold over the road so thickly that it's almost pitch-dark, even though the last drops of late afternoon sun are still dancing on the treetops. I can't see if Mama's car is in there.

I notice four deep slashes—almost like bear claw marks—in the bark of a tree trunk near the edge of the road. They're too straight to be caused by branches but not straight enough to be caused by an ax, and they're spaced unevenly. Then there's a flash deep in the trees, like someone lighting a campfire, but in a few moments it's gone. From somewhere far away I hear a sound between a shriek and a cackle. Paul and I jump.

"Probably some kind of bird," I tell him, shrinking into my seat to try to hide how much I'm shaking. "Or an owl."

"You can't go in those woods," he says.

"But Mama—"

"You don't even know if she's in there. And if she is, you can't help her if you're lost. Which you would be as soon as you left the road."

He's right. It's too dark and I don't have supplies for a trek in the woods.

"We'll go back for provisions," I say, using another of my favorite encyclopedia words. "A flashlight, water, maybe rope—"

"Rope?" Paul paces, hopping from the handle to my shoulder and back again. "Rope, she wants," he mutters. I ignore him as I struggle to roll us back up the hill.

A few minutes later, I'm in our room unzipping my backpack to load it with supplies when I hear the familiar rumble of our car. I have just enough time to stash the pack and curl up with one of Daddy's old books before Mama walks in.

There's a smudge of something red that looks like clay on her shirt, the smell of smoke—not cigarette smoke, but *campfire* smoke—and black blotches, along with something else, something I don't want to think about, on her jeans. Is it blood? Hers or someone else's?

"Now this is what I like to see," she says with a smile, dropping a kiss on the top of my head. I notice as she bends down that one of her earrings is missing. She scurries into the bathroom before I can get a long look at her.

"Where did you go?" I call after her. "Your clothes are a *mess*!"

Mama laughs through the half-open bathroom door. "You're one to talk, Miss I've-Been-Wearing-the-Same-Shirt-for-Three-Days."

"I like this shirt." I pat the fake-pearl snaps on the chest pocket. That pocket has a hole behind it, but it doesn't show. I can't say the same for the unraveling hem, but the fabric is worn so thin and soft it's like a second skin. Anyway, I'm not ready to let her off so easy. "What were you doing out there?"

"What were *you* doing in here?" Mama pops her head out of the door. Her hair swings loose, a dark curtain hiding the smudges on her face. "You know, I saw a girl about your age outside earlier. You should go and play with her."

"You can't just go and play with strangers, Ma. Besides, kids my age don't 'play' anymore."

She rolls her eyes. "Whatever you want to call it. Introduce yourself and then you're not strangers anymore, are you?" She tosses her hair back out of her face with a wild swish and ducks back into the bathroom.

When she returns, her cheeks have been scrubbed pink and her one earring has been put away. She's changed into her sweats and wiped away every trace of wherever it is she's been.

She settles on the bed next to me and asks me about my day. It's plain to see we're at a stalemate. She's not going to answer my questions and I'm not going to answer hers. I sigh and dive back into my book.

I WAKE TO THE SOUND OF STATIC. THE ROOM IS PITCH-DARK. AS my eyes adjust, I see that Mama is still fast asleep. The static is coming from the clock radio on the nightstand. The light behind the numbers is dim, almost burned out, but I can see that it says 3:27. Too early for Mama's alarm to go off.

Paul is still sleeping on the pillow. Anyway, he wouldn't be able to turn on the radio.

I slide out of bed and into my chair as quietly as I can. The needle on the radio rests right between ninety-nine and one hundred. Snatches of music slip in and out of the static, a twangy steel guitar and a piano that sounds like church music, two songs out of tune with each other.

I reach for the dial, but before I can turn it off, I hear voices, low and growly, like car wheels on gravel. At first

I can't make out words, only the rising and falling of sentences.

There's a hush. Even the static seems to get softer. Then a voice comes through clearly, so deep I can feel it in my bones.

THEY'RE COMING.

FIVE

I WAKE UP FOR THE SECOND TIME IN ONE MORNING, NOT TO THE radio but to the sounds of Mama getting ready.

When she sees that I'm awake, she sits down on the edge of my bed. "You slept late. I'm about to head out." She runs her hand through my bed-tangled hair, tucking a loose chunk of it behind my ear. "Remember when I said there would be nights I'd be gone working on a little side project? Well, tonight'll be the first of those nights."

She doesn't mention the static; I guess she slept through it. But I know what I heard. I stayed up for an hour more to see if I could hear the voice again, but I didn't.

I try to shake it from my mind and focus on the present. I don't need Mama more worried about me than she already is. "You're going to the same place you went last night?"

"Full of questions again, aren't we?" She smiles and dodges out of my way as I prop myself up on an elbow.

"I just wanna know what you're doing out there." I sound like a pouting kid, but I don't care. "And why you still don't have a uniform." She's wearing jeans, boots, and a Carhartt coat that looks way too heavy for Georgia in early autumn.

"It's coming," Mama says dismissively as she zips up the coat. "But I don't need one for this project, anyway. Better to just wear work clothes." She tugs on the hood on the back of her coat and shakes the ends of her hair loose over her shoulders. "Anyway, there's a chance I'll be home for dinner, but I probably won't be back till morning. I'll call and let you know. Plus, you have my number, and Miss Mavis can check in."

"I won't need her to."

"Well, she lives right behind the office if you need help. I'll leave you with her number, too."

"Okay," I say.

She ruffles the hair she just straightened and smiles at me as she stands up. "Make up your bed when you get out of it," she says. "I'm a maid, but I'm not *your* maid."

"Yes, Mama."

After she leaves and I grab a cereal bar for breakfast, I kneel next to the nightstand. The clock radio is still turned off. I switch it on and inch the dial carefully with my thumb until the needle is right where it was last night, between ninety-nine and one hundred. There's a country song playing, something slow and sad. Like what the wind through the trees would sound like if it were music.

I push the needle so it's closer to the one hundred than the ninety-nine. Now I hear religious music. Not the kind the cantor sang at my grandparents' temple. Those songs sounded sacred to me, but they're more quiet, serious. This song has clapping and stomping and someone banging on the piano. The people singing are so off-key, it seems like some of them might be singing different tunes at the same time. But you can hear in their voices that this is sacred to them, too.

When I push the needle back toward the ninety-nine, the country song returns. I look at Paul, who's still stretching awake. "Come check this out."

I dig the edge of my fingernail into the grooves of the dial and inch it forward as slowly as I can, just enough that the needle stops squarely between ninety-nine and one hundred and we hear . . .

Nothing.

It's completely silent, like the radio isn't on. I check three times to make sure it is. Any closer to ninety-nine and we start hearing country, any closer to one hundred and the gospel music comes in. But there's a spot right in between where there is nothing at all.

"Bubkes," says Paul, peering irritably over the cliff of the bedspread.

"This is where it was last night," I say. "But just now when I turned the radio on, it was all the way over on a different channel."

Paul yawns. "Maybe your mama moved it."

"I don't think so. I think the radio turned *itself* on. And I think it set itself on that channel, and then switched to something else so nobody would know!"

"You're giving that radio a lot of credit for a hunk of plastic," he huffs.

I look over at the window, where the shades are parted enough that I can see the edge of those woods, dark even in the morning.

Paul curls into a ball on my shoulder as I unfold my book and settle down under the air conditioner. We stay like that for most of the morning and into the afternoon, until I start to feel hungry. I grab my chair by the footrest and pull it closer, slapping on the brakes so I can pull myself up into it. "Come on," I say. "Let's go find something to eat."

Soon we're parked in front of the vending machine. "Aren't you happy I brought you with me this time?"

"Ecstatic," says Paul. "Get the pretzels, they look fresher."

I look down the forbidden hill out of the parking lot.

I wonder how far town is and whether I could get there on my own four wheels. I wonder if there'll be any dinner before Mama disappears to whatever project is keeping her out all night, or if I'll have to make do with vending machine snacks.

Just then, out of the corner of my eye, I swear I see something move. I whip my head around, but it's just Miss Mavis's bony fingers dragging through her window blinds. One watery blue eye peers through a slit, then disappears.

Then I notice that whoever drew the hopscotch squares has gone over them with fresh neon chalk. The person who made them is still here. Maybe even *lives* here.

I catalog that thought on the way back to our room, but I don't investigate further. I've got a dead dad, a mom who cleans everyone else's rooms, an invisible dragon with a Yiddish accent, and a scar on my arm from being bullied. Not to mention I'm surrounded by creepy woods that eat people. I've got enough problems.

Inside the room, something feels out of place. It takes me a moment to notice a note and a few bills sitting on top of the TV.

Sorry I missed you, hon. I had to dash in and out on my break! Here's some money and the number for a pizza place in town. Call them for dinner. I'll be back in the morning. Love, Mama.

It's hard to see our room from the parking lot because it's around a bend in the motel. Still, for Mama to have come and gone in the short time I was out, she must have slipped in and out of the door quickly and quietly. Almost like she didn't *want* me to run into her.

I crumple the note into my pocket and roll to the window, pulling the curtains closed. I don't know how I didn't notice before. Mama's car isn't even *in* the parking lot.

SIX

I TRY SO HARD TO STAY AWAKE AS LONG AS I CAN THAT NIGHT.
And sure enough, just as my limbs start to feel like they're
filled with sand, a crackling pulls me from the edge of
sleep. Before I even look at the radio, I know the needle is
going to be between ninety-nine and one hundred.

There's a sound like rocks scraping together, a grind-
ing that doesn't quite cover the sound of distant howling.
I don't think it's the wind. Then, the same deep voice:
ALERT THE REST OF THE GUARDIANS.

I poke Paul. "Whaddaya want?" he mumbles.

"It's happening again," I whisper. "The radio."

WE MUST STOP THEM. BY ANY MEANS.

"Stop what?" I whisper. "Or . . . who? 'By any means'
sounds scary!"

He yawns. "It's probably just a radio play."

"A radio play?" That sounds like something from the
days before TV was invented.

"We're up in the mountains; maybe somebody's got a little station . . . people gotta keep themselves occupied, you know?"

"Why would they be performing plays in the middle of the night when everybody's sleeping? And why doesn't the radio station come in during the daytime?"

"I don't know. Radio isn't really my specialty. I've just been around long enough to know that when things seem weird, there's usually a good explanation. Can we go back to sleep now?"

"*You* can," I say. "I'm gonna stay up and figure this out."

I tuck the radio under my pillow and turn the volume down to where I can just barely hear it. If I keep it on, maybe I won't lose the station.

I try to make out what they're saying, but a lot of the words are too low to hear. I can barely make out *GUARD-IANS . . . BEASTS . . . WITCH OF THE WOODS . . .*

What's being guarded? By who? If it's a play, it doesn't make any sense. And . . . a *witch*? I bolt up at that word, not sure that's what I actually heard.

I can feel myself starting to slip in and out of sleep again. Just before I lose consciousness, the voices say: *THE GIANT.*

I OPEN MY EYES TO SUN STREAMING THROUGH THE PARTED CUR-tains. The room smells like hot buttered toast. My head is still fuzzy from waking up, so it takes a few minutes to register that Mama is talking on the phone, her back turned to me and her voice muffled.

I pull the quilt over my head. The light shines through the tacky flower print, making me feel like I'm under the trees in an especially ugly forest. I angle my head in Mama's direction so I can hear her better.

"It was a battle last night. There were so many of them." A pause. "I know," she says finally. "But the closer I get to the village, the harder they come. I might need . . ." she trails off. I hear faint rustling. "Hold on," says Mama. "I think she's awake."

I try to lie as still as possible, but it's too late.

"I'll have to call you back," Mama says, followed by the *click* of the receiver dropping back into its cradle.

A moment later, my flower canopy is whisked away, replaced by Mama's smiling face. "You fall asleep listening to music?" She points at the radio still tucked under my pillow.

"No, I . . ." I consider trying to explain the midnight radio station, but I don't know how not to make it sound like another wild story. Like Paul. The radio is turned off now, but I *know* I didn't turn it off. "Actually, I was listening to the radio. And I heard voices. I thought I heard someone say . . . *guardians*," I say finally. "Did you turn it off? Do you know what I'm talking about?"

For a split second, she pauses. An unreadable expression flits across her face, then she frowns. "No. You must have been dreaming. Or maybe you bumped it in your sleep?"

"Yeah." I sit up and pull the radio into my lap. "I'm sure that's what happened."

I fiddle with the dial, trying to get it to land between ninety-nine and one hundred. Just like last time, I get either twangy country or off-key gospel, but in between there's nothing but dead air.

Mama makes a face. "The reception's terrible up here."

I switch it off. "Do you know anything about a station that does, like, radio plays? But it only comes in in the middle of the night?"

"What? You were definitely dreaming."

I know I wasn't. But how do I convince anyone else? I give up and set the radio back down on the nightstand. "When did you get back?"

"A few hours ago. Looked like you just dropped out, lights on and everything. Didn't so much as stir when I put you to bed." She drops a bag on the nightstand. "I brought breakfast."

"Thanks." I pull food containers and plastic silverware out of the bag. If she went to the diner, she's been into town. Did she go this morning before I woke up? Or is that where she was all night? Is Windy Pines "the village"? If it is, why haven't I heard anyone else call it that? And who—or *what*—were there too many of there? The sight of whipped butter melting on top of thick blueberry pancakes makes my stomach rumble, and my attention shifts to the food.

Mama laces her work shoes.

"You're going in again?" I ask. "Aren't you still tired from last night?"

"A little," she says, sitting down on the bed. "But I'm off on Friday. What do you say we drive into town, explore? Get to know the place."

"That sounds fun."

After she leaves, I finish breakfast and get dressed, then wake Paul who has slept through everything. "I was up late standing guard," he explains, shaking out his scales like a bird might its feathers.

"Guard against what? And if something *did* come in here, what could *you* do about it? I'm a hundred times your size."

"There's no need to be rude," he says. "What's the point of a dragon that doesn't protect you?"

Breakfast has made me thirsty, so I decide to roll out to the vending machine for a soda. I'm feeling generous enough to let Paul hop in my pocket for the ride.

The chalk on the hopscotch squares is fresh again, and someone added rainbows, butterflies, and shooting stars with long, colorful tails. In the middle, in big bubble letters, it says: CHAPEL BELL. That seems like a strange thing to write, especially since I haven't heard a bell since we've been here. I make a mental note to listen for one in case it means something.

A lady in a flowered muumuu with curlers in her hair steps out of her room and gives me a long stare. I stick my tongue out at her and she huffs and goes back inside.

The thing is, I don't hate my chair. I love how much easier it is to get around with it compared to when I was still trying to walk. I love being able to go fast and do what I want instead of tiring easily.

But I hate the way *other* people react to it: the gawping and the comments, even from people who think they're being nice but who talk to me like I'm a little kid or a puppy. And then there's the bullying. Sometimes, like with Corinne, it's because they don't believe I really need the chair, but at other times they don't even get to know me enough to learn I *can* move my legs. They just see a person who's different and that's enough.

A dusty can of orange soda falls with a *clunk* into the machine's trough. I snake my hand through the little door to grab it, then turn around to find myself looking into the face of the hopscotch girl.

SEVEN

"HI!"

The girl, a little smaller than me with sparkling dark eyes in a heart-shaped brown face, her rows and rows of bead-adorned braids swinging around her shoulders, smiles and waves even though she's right in front of me. Deep dimples form in her cheeks. She's wearing purple overalls and a shirt with ruffly sleeves that look like tiny wings. I notice she has glasses with pale purple plastic frames, which makes me wonder if she owns objects in any other color. But I figure I'm not one to judge.

"Hi," I say, tucking the soda into the pocket of my jeans.

"I've seen you around," she says. "Your mama works here, right?"

"She does custodial work," I say, using the fancy word instead of *maid*. I consider telling her about the nights Mama does other stuff for Miss Mavis, but then I wonder if it's a secret. So I keep my mouth shut.

"Are you gonna be here for a while, then?" she asks. I realize we've started moving in the direction of the courtyard.

"Yeah," I say. "My mama says we're staying here for good."

"Here in the Giant? Or in Windy Pines?"

We've reached her hopscotch squares. She skips across them and back as she talks, landing in the field of rainbow stars.

"Both, probably," I say. "I think our room is part of the deal of Mama's job. Plus it's easy for me to get into." I nod down at my wheels.

"Oh," she says. "Yeah, I didn't think about that. Sorry."

"It's okay," I say. "There just aren't a lot of places that don't have stairs. You really don't notice until you can't get up them."

She nods. "Well, I like your chair. Pink is probably my second-favorite color."

I start to tell her I didn't choose the color, but that might sound like I'm insulting her. So I just say "Thanks." To change the subject, I point at the creepy angel under the palm tree. "Have you seen that?"

She follows my hand. "The Millie Dobbs stone?"

"I guess. I noticed the plaque. Who was Millie Dobbs?"

"I don't know her whole story. But there's a jump rope rhyme." She claps in rhythm as she chants. "*Millie Dobbs,*

Millie Dobbs, Daddy's in the forest chopping logs. Run back to town, don't make a sound—here you turn around while you're jumping," she says, demonstrating with an imaginary rope. *"Do you hear the wind or Millie's sobs?!"*

"Ugh." I shudder. "That makes her sound so creepy!"

The girl shrugs. "I guess so. But I like creepy things." She frowns and pulls a stubby stick of chalk out of her pocket, squatting to fix the smudged *B* on the hopscotch squares.

"What does that mean?" I ask.

"Hm?"

"What chapel bell? I haven't heard one since I've been here."

She starts laughing and stands up, dusting her palms off on her hips. *"I'm* Chapel Bell."

I stare at her. "You're the chapel bell?"

She shakes her head. "Not *the*. Chapel Bell is my name. My mother always liked the word *chapel* and thought it would make a pretty name. And then she married a man named Bell but didn't change her mind." She shrugs.

"Oh." My cheeks feel hot. "Sorry." I roll closer and put out my hand. "My name is Jerry Blum."

Chapel Bell looks at my hand for a minute like she's not sure what to do with it, then finally shakes it. I realize that introducing yourself with a handshake is probably not something normal kids do. She doesn't say anything about it, though.

"Are you?" I ask her. "Going to be here for a while, I mean?"

She nods and sits down on the steps. "Our house burned down. We're staying until my parents find us another place. There's all this stuff with the insurance company. I hear them talking about it sometimes when they think I'm not listening." She smiles. "I don't really mind staying here, though. I miss having my own room, but I like how there are always different people coming and going. Plus I think the motel might be haunted."

She says it so casually that I almost don't catch it at first. "Wait, what?"

"I love ghosts," she says. "Personally, I plan on being a ghost." She must see something in my face because she quickly adds, "Not right away, of course. I want to live a long life. But when I'm old and I die, I want to come back as a ghost. So I can watch everything happen after I'm gone. And the only people who'll be able to see me are people who are sensitive to ghosts, which is usually people who are *respectful* of ghosts."

"What about ghost hunters?" I say, thinking of those TV shows where people try to find ghosts and banish them back to the world of the dead.

"The real ghost hunters leave benevolent spirits alone if they want to stay," Chapel says authoritatively. *Benevolent* is one of the words I learned from my dictionary. It means friendly. "I'm planning on being a benevolent spirit. I don't want to hurt anyone. But I do want to haunt. I think it sounds fun. Harmless haunting, though."

"Do you think this place is harmlessly haunted?" I ask her. "Or are they, like, the *not*-so-benevolent spirits?"

"This place is old, and any place that's old probably has ghosts. But since lots of people have passed through here, that makes it more likely that there are multiple ghosts. Maybe different kinds of ghosts. I read a lot of ghost books—not just ghost *stories*, but books about real ghosts. And I can pick up on energies. I think I'm one of the sensitive ones. At least a little bit."

"Maybe I am, too," I say. That would explain some of the weird stuff happening around here.

She looks at me. "Why do you say that?"

I take a chance. "Have you heard the midnight radio station?"

"Is that a band?"

I shake my head. "Never mind."

"I haven't *seen* a ghost," Chapel admits. "But I can sometimes sort of sense shifts in the energy, and I think that might be them trying to be seen. Like maybe I'm not totally ready yet, but I'm trying to learn how to be *open* to seeing them, so they can show themselves."

"What if they show themselves, but they're not

benevolent?" I ask her. I remember the voices from the midnight radio. They didn't sound friendly to me.

She starts to answer, but a door opens and a man calls her name.

"Sorry, I gotta go! We'll talk more later, okay? It's good to meet you!"

"Yeah, okay," I say, as Chapel jumps to her feet and runs up the steps.

After I'm alone, I take a sip of soda and turn in the direction of my own room. "That was surprisingly okay," I mutter to myself. It helps push down the flutter of something like hope inside me. Meetings with other kids rarely start this well. But they *never* end well.

Something stops me before I can roll back inside: the neon sign above the office, blinking faintly in the sun. THE SLUMBERING GIANT.

Chapel called it the Giant, too. And then I remember the voice growling through the speaker last night saying the same thing. *The Giant.*

The voices weren't talking about a monster. They were talking about this place.

They were talking about us.

EIGHT

MAMA HAS TO WORK EARLY AGAIN THE NEXT DAY, BUT AT LEAST she brings me breakfast again. After she kisses me good-bye and I get dressed, I decide I might as well take a look around. If these creatures are somehow watching us, there have to be clues.

As soon as I roll out of our room, I notice a newspaper outside one of the other doors. There's a headline on the front page about Edwin Martinez, the disappeared logger.

I stoop forward for a closer look.

"That's like the third one this year," says a voice behind me.

I turn around to find Chapel Bell, wearing a purple sundress and a new collection of Band-Aids. "Hi again," she says.

"Hey," I say. "What do you mean, the third one?"

She shrugs. "There have always been stories of people going missing in the woods. I remember hearing them when I was little. But I thought they were just urban legends—well, rural legends, I guess—until lately all these real people have been going missing.

"Every year, a few loggers or Forest Service guys don't make it back from the season." Chapel keeps talking, skipping back and forth from one foot to the other. "And sometimes you'll hear about someone going in there hiking or camping—out-of-towners, probably, I don't know anyone who would go in there for fun—and they don't come back when they're supposed to, so there's a search party. Once there was a whole Boy Scout troop."

Something scratches at my brain as I stare at the logger's picture.

"Is there a library around here?" I blurt, turning to face Chapel. She stops skipping and takes a step back, blinking in surprise.

"Sure there is," she says. "It's in town, though. Probably too far to walk—I mean, roll." She gestures at my chair with a sheepish expression.

"It's okay," I say. I can't stand people making a big deal out of apologizing for mistakes like that. Like they can't stop calling attention to it. It's somehow worse than leaving me out in the first place.

Chapel has already moved on. She jumps up. "I've got it! We can ask my dad for a ride when he goes into town for groceries." She nods in the direction of an old pickup truck parked in the lot. "Your chair would fit in the back. Maybe I can even talk him into leaving now!"

We? "Wait—" I start, but Chapel is already clanging up the metal steps to her room.

A moment later, the door swings open and Chapel skips back down the steps, followed by a tall man with a boyish face despite his mustache. Like Chapel, he wears glasses, but his are black and horn-rimmed. "This is my dad," Chapel announces, gesturing toward him with a flourish. "Daddy, this is Jerry."

Mr. Bell smiles at me, carving dimples just like Chapel's into his cheeks. "Hello, Jerry," he says. He doesn't do that thing of staring at me for a beat too long, trying to make sense of my boy name and my pink chair and my dad's shirts and my salad-bowl hair.

I decide I like him.

Chapel hops into the pickup while Mr. Bell helps me onto the edge of the seat and carefully puts my chair in the bed of the truck. Chapel slides into me, squishing me against the door as her dad throws the truck bumpily into gear. She giggles like the whole thing is fun.

I can feel her skin against mine. I can't remember the last time I've been this close to anyone besides Mama or Paul, who don't really count. As we roll away from the motel, she scoots back a little, enough that I'm not jammed up against the glass anymore, but not so much that we're not still touching.

We stay like that all the way into town, which really isn't that far. A few minutes past the motel parking lot, the dirt roads start to thin out, replaced by small houses, a trailer park, a gas station.

The center of town is a single stoplight strung across the middle of a four-way intersection. There's a bank, a small supermarket, a hardware store, the pizza place, and a diner. A few more stores are scattered along the road, but I can't read their signs. Some look boarded up, with empty, trash-strewn parking lots and burned-out neon tubes circling their marquees like dead snakes. All of it stands in the shadow of a huge old building covered with chutes and pulleys.

We pull to a stop in front of the Windy Pines Public Library, which doesn't look like a typical library. Instead, it's a double-wide mobile home on stilts. The only things marking it as a library are the flags out front and a book drop that resembles a dumpster. In fact, I'm pretty sure it *is* made out of an old dumpster and somebody just painted the words "book drop" on the side.

"This is it?" I say as Mr. Bell unloads my chair. At least it has a ramp.

"It's bigger on the inside," Chapel says with a huge grin. She keeps looking at me like she expects me to laugh or say something in response, but I don't get it.

As I roll myself after her, she skips up the ramp talking about a TV show with an alien that flies around in a time-traveling telephone box that's bigger on the inside than it appears. I only halfway understand her, but when we get inside, I see what she means. The trailer is stacked floor to ceiling with shelves of books that make it seem like it holds a lot more than it looks like it would.

Chapel grabs a note card and a stubby pencil and starts circling the shelves, scribbling down call numbers and pulling down reference books until she has a tall stack in her arms. Meanwhile, I make a beeline for the library's only computer and drag a rolling chair aside so I can park my wheelchair in front of it. By the time I access the internet, Chapel has come over.

She peers over my shoulder at the screen. "You're not gonna find much about Windy Pines there," she says. "We're too small. Nobody cares about us unless they're coming up from Atlanta or down from Chattanooga looking to get scared because of the ur—*rural* legends." She reaches around and types something into the address bar, and an ancient-looking HTML message board pops up. The lime-green type on a purple background is hard to read, but I quickly learn that it's a page where people report sightings of strange creatures or supernatural phenomena.

I scroll past several entries about the Jersey Devil and the sunken city under Lake Lanier before I see the name of Windy Pines jump out under the headline "The Shadow Demons of North Georgia."

"No way," I murmur.

Behind me, Chapel softly reads out loud. "'The disappearances coincide'—that means they happen at the same time—'with reported sightings of the demons, who hide in the hills in old coal mines. According to those who've seen them, the demons resemble shadows that move and take on a shape of their own: solid creatures with sharp claws and teeth that move through the woods like smoke. They hide in the trees and in the mines among the coal deposits. Some have reported seeing fires near the former mines.'"

Fires. I remember seeing what I could have sworn were flames through the trees around the motel.

Chapel spins around to face me, her eyes wide. "Jerry, demons!" She twists her fingers nervously, as if a demon might walk into the room. "I mean, I was always *sure* there were ghosts, but demons are a different level."

"You really believe this stuff?" Even with the weirdness going on around here, these stories seem far-fetched. Like what you'd say to scare people around a campfire.

"I believe in everything," Chapel replies. "Or at least, the *possibility* of everything. If it hasn't been proven to not exist, how can I say for sure it doesn't?"

What she's saying makes a certain kind of sense. If all these things are happening that nobody can explain, could it be that they're not looking for the right explanations? But still . . .

"Does it say anything about the Guardians?" I ask.

Chapel's nose scrunches. "Guardians of what?"

Before she can answer, I sense someone behind us. We turn to see a librarian, an older woman with a short, broad body, an elegant gray twist, and a not-unkind face with lightly wrinkled brown skin. "Pardon me, but I noticed you two seem to be looking for old newspapers. I can show you where to search the articles if you'd like."

By the time Mr. Bell's truck rattles into the parking lot, we've read dozens of newspaper articles on the microfiche machine the librarian showed us how to use, articles too old and too local for anyone to have bothered putting on the internet. We've printed out stories from the message board and photocopied pages from the thick, dusty local history books Chapel found. I know more than I even wanted to know about demons, but I still have no idea what the Guardians are.

I don't want to let on how worried I am about Mama. But most of what we find sound like Halloween myths. There are stories of demons hiding in abandoned mine shafts and hoarding treasure and descriptions of the magic powers they're said to have, powers that can weaken and confuse people through touch.

On one of the posts, though, somebody left a comment that sticks in my mind: *I heard the town is guarded against the demons. But that doesn't make it safe.*

NINE

LATER THAT AFTERNOON, I'M SITTING ON THE BED, TRYING TO figure out how to tell Mama about the voices on the radio and the demon stories and the fact that I just met a girl who senses strange energy in this place in a way that *won't* sound like a wild story when she comes in, hours earlier than she's supposed to.

"Are you on break?" I ask.

She shakes her head. "Remember the other night when I had to go and do the—the special work?"

"Yes." I don't like the way she's talking about it. Like there's something she's trying not to say. It makes me think about how Chapel Bell's parents only discuss their burned-down house when they think she's not listening. Sometimes I wish parents would realize it doesn't make scary things easier when they try to hide them from you.

"Well, I gotta do it again tonight. It's a little short notice. I'm sorry about that. I feel like I've been gone the entire time we've been here."

I nod. "It's okay."

"No, it's not," she says. "But it's the way it has to be. I'll leave you pizza money again."

I scoot toward the edge of the mattress. "But what about you?"

"What do you mean?"

I notice what she's wearing again: thick jeans, heavy boots, layered work shirts under a farm coat (even though it's seventy degrees outside). These are clothes you wear to protect yourself. They're armor. "I'm worried about you," I say. "I don't know if this town is safe, Mama. There are weird things happening."

"Baby, every town has its weird things. That's just what makes a place interesting." She bends down to tie the laces on her boots, then straightens up and pulls her hair back. "I promise I'll be safe."

She pulls a twenty-dollar bill out of her wallet and tucks it into my shirt pocket right where Paul is napping. "Hey!" he shouts. I clap my hand over my pocket to shush him.

Mama looks at me like she knows. There's a certain weariness in her face when she says, "You know the drill. Miss Mavis is right over there"—she nods at the wall as if we can see through the ugly wallpaper to the office—"if you need anything. You can always call her for help, okay?"

"Okay," I say, even though to be honest, Miss Mavis

creeps me out just as much as everything else around here. I don't feel better knowing she's right through the wall, but I know Mama feels like she's not leaving me alone, so I don't say anything.

She starts to put her wallet away, then seems to reconsider. She grabs a few singles and hands those to me, too. "For the vending machine," she says. "Just in case."

After she leaves, I leaf through the printouts from the library. The newspaper stories don't say much about demons or guardians, but townspeople keep repeating the word *cursed*. I shiver and tuck them at the back of the stack.

Apparently Windy Pines used to be a mining camp and after that dried up, a mill town, a well-off one at that. I guess the hulking, half-collapsed building on the far side of town is what's left of the mill. Once it shut down, nothing else brought in money or jobs, and the town kind of fell apart. That accounts for all the boarded-up shops and abandoned houses and rusted-out trailers. Even this motel was built when there was a reason people wanted to come here. Now it only attracts guests who don't have a choice.

The disappearances seem to have started in the mill days, becoming more and more frequent until it shut down. They stopped as the logging roads grew over with brush. But over the last few years, people began logging the woods again, and as soon as they did, loggers started going in and not coming out.

I'm comforted by the thought that mostly loggers are going missing. I'm pretty sure Mama couldn't be a logger and keep it a secret. Until I turn the page and see a faded black-and-white photo of a pretty girl with long dark hair. She's wearing an old-fashioned dress with a big white collar and a pendant with an antique-looking stone shaped like a heart that almost seems to shimmer around her neck. *Millie Dobbs,* I read. *Ten-year-old daughter of logging foreman Walter Dobbs. Ventured into the woods in May 1933 and never returned.*

My hands shake. The papers slip through my fingers and drop into my lap. I recognize that name from the motel. "The angel," I whisper.

I read on. Millie's family was one of the most prominent in Windy Pines, and her disappearance shook the whole town. They searched for months but she was never found. Finally, her father dedicated a statue in her memory near the woods she loved on the site of what is now the Slumbering Giant Motel. It seems like Millie was the first to go missing; the loggers started vanishing not long after that.

I can't read anymore. I fold over the paper with Millie's photo and tuck it into the middle of the stack, letting the other stories swallow her. Then I slide the stack under the bed and drop the bedspread down to hide them away.

TEN

I WAIT TO ORDER PIZZA UNTIL IT'S ALMOST DARK. THE PARKING lot is starting to take on that eerie look it gets when headlights reflect off the blacktop. Millie's angel stands sentry in the middle, the tips of its wings casting shadows even darker than those descending from the sky. I shiver and let the curtain fall back over the window.

The driver shows up maybe half an hour after I call. It's the same guy as last time, and his brow scrunches up like a bushy caterpillar as he hands me the pizza box through the car window. "Are you in there all alone?"

"No, I'm out here all alone," I say. "Don't even have a room. I was left all by myself in this parking lot with nothing but pizza money."

At this point, the driver starts to look more angry than concerned. "I'm okay," I tell him. "Promise." I put the box in my lap and wheel myself back toward the motel as he drives away.

"Hey."

The voice sounds like it's hovering in the air and I start to wonder if maybe there *are* ghosts haunting this motel. Then I see Chapel sitting on the catwalk that connects the upper rooms, her legs dangling through the slats of the railing. She waves.

"Hey." I wave back. My stomach drops like I'm going over that first big hill on a roller coaster. It's a feeling that comes with knowing something I'm about to do is a big, scary risk, but that I'm going to do it anyway.

Then I lift the pizza box. "I was just going to eat this in my room. Want some?"

"Sure! Let me ask my parents."

I wait, the warmth from the pizza box spreading across my thighs. My eyes drift over to the tree line. In the dusk, the outlines of the nearest branches are visible, but beyond that there's nothing but darkness.

Then I see a glow coming from deep in the trees, like someone's lit a fire. Who would be camping in those creepy woods? It's too late for loggers to be there. Another flash of light interrupts my thoughts, quick and bright like the last one, but coming from even deeper within. Dancing around the lights are tiny ember-red flickers, like red fireflies. I blink and it's all gone.

The door slams and Chapel comes running back out. "They said it's okay," she says after she lands next to me. "I just have to be back by nine."

"Great." I give a last shivering glance back at the woods—dark now, as if the lights were never there—and we head back to my room.

I set the pizza box down on the bed as Chapel looks around. "So this is your room."

"Yeah," I say. "Is it different from yours?"

"Not really. But instead of that horse painting"—she points at a frame hanging over the beds—"we have one with a lighthouse. And our bedspreads are blue."

She sits on one edge of my bed and I roll around to the other side, park my chair, and climb up next to her. "Their pizza is pretty good," I say. "Have you had it?"

She shakes her head. "My dad still cooks most of our food. We have a hot plate and a toaster oven in our room. It's not fancy, but he's a really good cook, so the food tastes almost as good as it did when we had a real kitchen."

My own pizza slice is almost to my lips when thinking about Chapel's house stops me from taking a bite. "It was in town, right?" I say. "Your house?"

"Yeah, over by the post office. My mama actually wanted to rebuild another house on the same lot. But Daddy talked her into selling it. He wants to buy a farm on the other side of town so we can raise goats and chickens like he did growing up."

I think about the farms we passed on the outskirts of

town, how one of them could belong to Chapel's family. I picture her feeding the animals, gathering eggs for her daddy to cook in a big farmhouse kitchen. It makes me happy and sad at the same time. I know we barely know each other, but even still. Will she even remember me once she has her new life?

Then I have another memory. When Mama and I first drove into town, we passed the middle school. I could feel her slowing down the car even as I dug my nails into the armrest on the door, willing it to go away. She was expecting me to be excited to see kids my own age, and I couldn't stand the thought of telling her the truth, of sinking her hopeful smile.

It must have been lunchtime because there were clusters of kids outside. Groups of kids, especially giggling kids, make me nervous. On some level, I know it's probably not me they're laughing at, but I've been conditioned to hear laughter as a warning bell. If they *are* bullies, they'll laugh right before they attack.

"Did you go to the school out there?" I ask Chapel.

"The middle school? I still do." That explains why I don't always see her during the day. "I just started sixth grade. What grade are you in?"

"I'm in sixth, too," I say. I mean, I *would* be. If I went to regular school. It's not really a lie.

Her eyes narrow. "But you don't go to school here." It's not a question. There's only one middle school in town. She would have seen me there.

"No, not—not yet." I don't feel like explaining the whole "homeschooled" thing to the only person my age who doesn't treat me differently because of my chair.

Fortunately, Chapel doesn't push it. We sit on my bed and eat the pizza and watch an old black-and-white movie about a haunted house. She's seen it before. She's seen everything that has a ghost in it.

The movie ends right at nine o'clock, so she says good night and hops back up the steps to her room. I close the box on the last couple of cold slices and set it on top of the dresser before I roll myself to the shower.

When I get back, Paul is waiting. "What was that all about?" he asks.

"What was what about?"

"All the hemming and the hawing and dodging the subject of going to school in town." He prances around the edge of the bed. "You finally got a friend, and you still don't wanna go?"

"I never wanted to go," I say. "And we're not friends, not like that."

"Sure looked that way to me," he says. "But what do I know? I watched the evening from a drawer."

I ignore him as I roll to the bed and turn back my bedspread. After I'm lying down with the covers over me, I speak. "She's really nice. But she goes to a regular school and has regular friends, and she's going to move out of the motel and get a farm and have a regular life. And maybe that'll be months from now or maybe it'll be days, but I'm better off with it being you and me. Friends complicate things."

Paul sighs and climbs onto the pillow next to me. "Do you remember how we became friends?" he says. "Before that, *you* had a regular house, regular school, regular friends."

I think of my old school in our old town, when my dad was still alive and we still had our house and I didn't need my chair yet. I had friends. Chase and Reyna and Samira. None of them were ever mean to me, but they started joining sports and clubs like the dance team that I couldn't be in. And it wasn't like they stayed together and left me behind; it's just that they all kind of went in different directions. We stopped being a group, which Mama said was normal as people grow up. But they all found new friends in their new groups and I just *didn't*. And then my dad died and it was like nobody knew what to say to me, so everybody stopped talking to me. And then we left.

"You found me when you felt your most alone," Paul

says. "But it's okay to *not* be alone. You gotta take a chance on letting other people in."

"Okay," I say, because I'm too tired to argue. I roll over and reach up to switch off the light.

"Note I said *people*," comes Paul's voice through the darkness.

"Okay."

ELEVEN

WHEN I WAKE UP, IT TAKES ME A FEW MINUTES TO REGISTER THAT
something is wrong. The lights are still off, and nobody
has opened the blackout shades, so the room is too dark
to match the time on the clock radio: 9:53 a.m. Too late
for me to be just waking up. Mama should already be at
work. Did she come back and leave without waking me?
She never does that.

Her bed is perfectly made. There's no takeout bag with
breakfast, no note on top of the TV. Nothing to indicate
she's been here.

I throw back the covers and poke Paul awake. He jerks
up with a snort that sends puffs of flameless smoke into
the air. "Mama's not here," I say.

"So? She shouldn't be here at this time of the morning.
She probably got back late and didn't want to wake you
up."

"That's what I thought at first, but . . . look around. She didn't leave anything. She didn't even open the curtains, and she always does that. I don't think she's been here."

Paul yawns. "Maybe she's not back yet."

"Maybe not, but I'm starting to get worried. I'm gonna go talk to Miss Mavis." I'm not sure how she can help, but I have to do *something*. She's the one who sent Mama out to do whatever it is she was doing last night.

I shrug on some clothes without looking to see if they match. As I pass the mirror, I catch a glimpse of my reflection; my hair is sticking up in the back. I try to smooth it down, but I don't have much success and after a couple of tries I give up.

The office looks quiet and empty. I find a small hidden latch on the gate that runs behind the office, push it open, and wheel myself down the narrow walkway that leads to Miss Mavis's room. The TV inside is blaring one of those daytime game shows where people dress in silly costumes and yell a lot. I knock.

"Hold yer horses!" she yells, even though I knocked only once. "I'm comin'!"

The door snaps open a few inches. "Jerusha!"

"Jerry," I correct her.

"Jerry," she repeats. "Couldn't you get into the office?"

I have to bite back the question of how, if I couldn't get

through an unlocked door to get into the office, it would somehow have been easier to unlock a gate barely wider than my chair and roll myself down a path *not quite* as wide as my chair.

"No ma'am, I didn't have any trouble getting in," I say. "I just thought I'd get to you faster if I came back here." Once it's out of my mouth, I wonder if it sounds too sassy, but she doesn't seem upset. In fact, a small smile twitches at the corners of her mouth.

"Well, come on in," she says.

Her apartment is dark and the carpet is as thick as moss. It's hard to wheel across, but I try not to show it. On TV, a lady in a chicken suit is spinning a wheel with glittery numbers painted all around it.

"Did you need help with something, sweetheart?" Miss Mavis asks.

"No, I'm just—I'm looking for my mom," I say. "I thought you might know where she is."

"She didn't tell you?" Miss Mavis shuffles into the kitchen. The carpet gives way to cracked linoleum near Miss Mavis's stove and the sound changes from a shuffle to a scrape. "Want some tea?"

I'm already shaking my head *no* as she pours steaming reddish-black liquid into two mismatched teacups. She hands me one and I start to refuse, but I change my mind.

I suspect she's wondering if I can hold my own cup. I don't want to give her any signals she might take as confirmation.

"Your mama," Miss Mavis says after a long sip of her tea, "is doing some extra work, mostly at night."

"I know about that," I say. "But she didn't come back this morning. I'm worried."

Miss Mavis nods. "These jobs," she says slowly. "They sometimes just take a night, sometimes a little longer. She'd be in touch if anything was wrong, but you're welcome to stay with me until she comes back."

"No," I blurt. Miss Mavis's eyes widen but she doesn't say anything. "I mean, no, thank you, ma'am. I don't need anyone to take care of me. I just need to know she's okay." I gulp down the rest of my tea and set the empty cup on her coffee table.

Miss Mavis has that look adults get when they're not going to tell you something they don't think you're ready to hear. It's the same look Mama got when I was five and read an unfamiliar word on a machine in a public bathroom, and no matter how hard I pressed she wouldn't tell me what a tampon was. "I think I should be going," I say. "Thank you for the tea."

"I'll let you out," she says, as if she's not sure about me being okay but also isn't sure how to argue. "If you need me, you know how to find me."

I wheel past her and into the sun, so bright in contrast to her dark living room that it makes me squint and shield my eyes.

In her doorway, Miss Mavis has a satisfied look on her face, like I've passed a test I never agreed to take. There isn't time to think about what it means.

I've got bigger things to do.

TWELVE

THERE'S SOMETHING I TOOK FROM OUR HOUSE WHEN MAMA AND
I hit the road. Before he died, Daddy had kept it in a safe
place in his room, a place I knew to sneak it from before
everything was cleared out.

Now I push on my brakes and slide down to the floor.
I lift the heavy bedspread and slide the leather case into
my lap. It has that old, warm smell I remember. Inside,
gleaming on a bed of dark blue velvet, is my dad's sword.
It's about as long as my arm and almost as wide, narrowing
to a very sharp point.

Daddy had been into fantasy books, ones with dragons
and elves and flaming swords and axes on the covers. I
remember him showing me the sword, taking it out carefully with the blade pointed away from us. "Someday,
maybe, you can hold it," he'd say. "But you have to learn to
respect it first. It's not a toy. It's a dangerous weapon."

"Why do you have a weapon?" I asked him.

"In case the trolls come," he said, smiling. "When you hear creaking in the night, it's the trolls coming to take you under the bridge so they can turn you into a troll, too. Then you'll spend the rest of your life holding bridges up like they do." Daddy blew on the tip of the sword like it was hot. "But I'm ready to defend you."

Mama had snorted later when I told her. "Your father bought that thing at a Renaissance fair. It's a nice piece of art, but it's just pretend."

Carefully, I take the sword out of the case. It's heavier than it looks. I touch the point of the blade with the very tip of my finger and wince. The sword might be just for decoration, but that doesn't mean it's not real.

I put it carefully on my lap, then stuff Mama's flashlight into my backpack. Even though it's still light outside, I'm not taking any chances.

It's now five p.m. and she's still not home. I've been waiting here all day. If I want answers, I'm going to have to find them on my own.

I figure Mama must have a reason for wearing such heavy clothes, so I choose my thickest pair of jeans, two of Daddy's flannel shirts, and his denim jacket. It has burn marks from the cigarettes he smoked, cigarettes I wouldn't even know about if not for those burns because he always smoked outside. Mama looked at those burn marks and only saw the cigarettes that caused them, but I always thought they symbolized how much he cared about me.

The jacket's so worn that there's a huge hole over the right chest pocket. Daddy had patched it himself, badly, with an old red bandanna. I touch my fingers to the cloth as I shrug it on. I'm carrying so much of him; I just hope it's enough to protect me.

I slip vending machine food—granola bars, trail mix, and bottled water—into the backpack. Then I remember the portable radio Daddy gave me for my birthday after I'd complained that I couldn't stream music without a phone. It's the one thing that makes me glad I'm not allowed to have one.

I find it, turn it on, and put on the headphones, adjusting the dial until it's right between ninety-nine and one hundred. Nothing but dead air. Still, I have a feeling the midnight radio station has something to do with Mama's disappearance. If it comes on when I'm searching for her, I'll be ready. I tuck the radio into my right pocket and unbutton the other one, motioning for Paul to climb in.

"No way," he says. "Nothing about this mishegas is safe."

"It's not about being *safe*," I tell him. "It's about saving my family."

"Why don't you at least tell Miss Marple? Or the girl upstairs?"

"Miss *Mavis*," I correct him, "thinks I'm a kid who can't handle myself. And even if I thought getting Chapel involved in this was a good idea—which, for the record, I don't—I think she's at some after school activity. And I can't wait around for her to get back."

He crosses his arms and puffs himself up to his full height. Which isn't much, but since he's on the bed and I'm in my chair, he's looking down at me. "And what if I refuse?"

I glare into his eyes. "Then I'll go by myself."

He stands firm for a moment longer, but he blinks first. "I'm not getting in your pocket," he grumbles, climbing onto my push handle and wrapping his tail around it.

THIRTEEN

THE THING ABOUT THE SLUMBERING GIANT'S PARKING LOT IS that you can always tell where the cars have been. Red mud from the road clings to the tires and leaves a trail stamped with the pattern of their treads. Where Mama's car had been parked, there's a set of tracks with a half-bald zigzag pattern and rainbow-colored drops of oil. The low-hanging sun glimmers on the drops, turning them into a trail of lights leading away from the motel. I follow them out of the lot.

When we get to the top of the hill, I see that the mud has washed across the road and the tracks have thickened. Keeping my eyes on Mama's oil-drip pattern, I release my brakes and slowly ease up on my wheels, sliding down the hill and away from the motel.

As the ground flattens, I notice the first road disappearing into the woods. The roadbed is raw red clay, muddy from the recent rain. I picture my wheels sinking into it.

Then a quick movement catches the corner of my eye, something too small to be a person but too purposeful to be an animal. It's like a moving shadow, wispy and shapeless. Probably nothing. I shake my head and it's gone.

We pass more logging trails, some of them wide enough for a truck and some too narrow for a person. I'm still on the asphalt, though the red clay gums up my wheels and slows me down. Because there's more mud here, the tire tracks are harder to tell apart. But that little rainbow shimmer lets me know that I'm still following Mama's car.

Until, suddenly, it doesn't.

I'm several feet past the last turnoff when I realize that I don't see the oil drips anymore. I pause, then turn around and start rolling back in the direction I came.

"What, you drop something?" Paul asks.

"Mama's car had an oil leak. It left a trail. And I don't see it anymore. I have to retrace our path back to where it stops."

"An oil leak? She really should get that fixed. Environmental concerns aside, the damage that can do to an engine—"

"Not the time, Paul," I say through gritted teeth.

I keep my eyes on the tracks. In a few places, I think I might see a zigzag, but nothing solid enough to trace. It's starting to seem like Mama's car was lifted into space, but then something sparkles in the mud ahead. As we get closer, I can tell it's where the oil trail ends. Or rather, where it *bends*. Because once I get to the little shiny puddle, I notice more dots of oil in the mud on the road's left side.

"She turned down here."

Paul snorts. "I don't even see how a car could get through there."

The trail is barely as wide as our car and it looks like it gets narrower the farther it goes, though the forest swallows it before I can see much. But there are tire tracks. And Mama's oil drips shine enough that I can see them glinting far into the trees.

I turn off the paved road right into the mud, which immediately sucks at my tires and slows me down. I steer toward the tracks, deep enough that there are puddles in them, but the mud at the bottom is packed hard and I can get some traction. It's getting darker as we go, the trees thickening overhead, and the constant howling of the wind is punctuated here and there by the hoot of an owl or a caw of a crow.

I hear other sounds, too. Small things skittering that I try not to think about. Deeper, murkier noises that I tell myself are the wind. There are rumbles under the brush, the snarl and snap of something much bigger than a squirrel or a possum.

This is where the loggers disappeared, the same woods my own mama told me not to mess with. But I keep my eyes on the shiny spots and drag my wheels deeper and deeper in. I'm so focused that at first I don't notice the oil spots veering off course. Until one lands right in front of me.

I look up and shine my flashlight ahead. Just a few feet in front of us, parked at a precarious tilt, is Mama's station wagon.

But she's not inside.

FOURTEEN

IN THE MOVIES AN ABANDONED CAR IS USUALLY ACCOMPANIED by signs of trouble: steam pouring from a grill, long scratches along the side, blood on the door handles. But Mama's car sits untouched, perfectly intact. Somehow, that doesn't make me feel relieved.

The driver's-side door is unlocked. After pushing on my brakes, I shift out of my chair and into the seat behind the wheel.

"Whaddaya doing?" Paul says. "You can't drive!"

"Looking for clues." I pop open the glove compartment. The door drops down heavily, spitting out registration papers, napkins from drive-throughs, a pack of gum. . . .

"Wait, what's this?" It's an old gas station map of Windy Pines that looks way too beat-up for Mama to have just bought it. "That's strange."

I hold up one end, letting it fall open into my lap. The yellow looks like it was made with a highlighter pen, marking lines coming out from a blue ballpoint star. I squint at the faded type next to the star. "That's the Giant!"

Paul jumps into the car and scoots across the seat to me. "What Giant? Where?"

I point to the star. "The Slumbering Giant. The motel. That star marks the Giant, and these yellow lines . . ." I trace my finger down the web of highlighter trails. "These are the logging roads. We're probably on one of them now!"

Paul leans in closer. "Which one?"

"I'm not sure. I wish I'd thought to count turnoffs from the top of the hill." I use the scale at the bottom of the map to measure the distance and figure it's just short of three miles from the Slumbering Giant to the center of town. I know I haven't rolled that far. "We're probably on about the third or fourth trail."

"Some of these go pretty deep in there," he notes. "You want me to get the flashlight?" Without waiting for an answer, he jumps back out of the car and with a little bit of effort drags the flashlight over.

"Hey, how'd you know you could do that?" As long as I've known Paul, I've never seen him move an object. How could he, when I made him up?

Paul shrugs. "I just knew. There's something different about the energy in here." A shudder runs down his tiny spine, twitching his whole body as he tries to shake it off.

"I'm not sure I like it."

With a shrug of my own, I switch the flashlight on and shine it into the trees. The thin cone of light doesn't show me how far the trail goes. I shine it on the dashboard instead, lighting up a panel of switches and knobs. "Any idea how to turn the lights on in this thing?" I tug on a handle next to the wheel. The windshield wipers come on, squeaking as they drag across the dry glass.

I reach across the wheel for another button and accidentally lean my elbow against the horn. It's Paul's turn to jump now. "Cripes!"

From the forest around us, I hear scurrying and flapping, and some kind of bird or small rodent cries out.

There's a knob a few inches down that pops open an ashtray. In my frustration, I slap it shut, and my hand slaps a nearly hidden button next to it. The woods ahead of us flood with light.

The trail ahead narrows sharply. Mama parked the car here because she *couldn't* drive any farther. My light bounces off boot prints on the ground, and I swing my legs sideways and line my own feet up with them. They're exactly where Mama's feet would have landed if she'd stepped out of the car.

I study the pattern of tiny interlocking diamond shapes in the boot tread. "We can follow these from here."

I pick up the map again. The third trail from the motel seems to intersect a bridge, one we never crossed. The next trail, though, is much shorter. Short enough that it's probably only wide enough to drive partway down. "We're right here." I point to the end of the yellow highlighter streak that continues where the road leaves off. "That must be where she's going."

"And what are all these?" Paul points at scattered *X*s around the map. Most of them are near, though not quite directly *on*, the yellow lines.

"I don't know." This map seems important. Why would Mama leave it behind? I notice what's written along the ridge of the mountainside, deep in the forest of green dots. GUARDIANS.

My mouth falls open. "She knows about the Guardians! When I asked her about the radio, she acted like she didn't! Why wouldn't she *tell* me?" I'm so upset that I drop the map, my hands shaking. As I'm picking it back up, a piece of paper falls out of the folds.

The handwriting isn't Mama's. It's tiny, crabbed cursive, hard to read, especially in the dim light, but I can make out some of the words.

"'A ring of stone will . . . trap the beast,'" I read. "'The charm is cast, the spirit released.'" I lower the note and look at Paul. "It's a poem."

"Sounds kinda woo-woo to me." He wrinkles his snout.

"Well, like it or not, it's our only clue so far." I squint at the paper again. "'Commit these markings to your . . . *hint*'? What does that word say?"

"Let me see." He crawls into my lap and picks up the paper. "This handwriting is awful!" He pauses. "Mind!" he finally says.

"'Commit these markings to your mind, then leave this map of shafts behind,'" I read.

"So Mama left the map on purpose," I say at the same time that Paul says, "Wait, what shafts?"

"Mine shafts. Those *X*s are old mine shafts. They must be," I whisper, thinking of the stories from the cryptid website. Demons lying in wait in their underground treasure stashes. "My mother," I say slowly, "is going after demons." For once, Paul doesn't disagree with me.

"What's the charm, then?" he asks. "It said there was a charm."

"I don't know," I admit. "The page just stops." I hold it up so he can see where the bottom is torn away.

I do my best to fold the map and slip it into my backpack but I keep the flashlight out. I don't think it's my imagination that the sky has darkened.

"Whaddaya *doin'*?" Paul demands. "It said right there in that . . . poem, or whatever it was, to leave this verkakte map behind!"

"Look, whatever the risks are of bringing it, it's safer than getting lost in the woods!" I shiver. "Especially after dark." I swear I hear something howl from in the trees.

I fold what's left of the paper and tuck it into my pocket. I'm saving if for when we find Mama.

If we find her.

FIFTEEN

AS WE ROLL ON, I TRY NOT TO FOCUS ON THE TRACKS AHEAD—those made by creatures that don't wear shoes. I don't know if I'm more scared that they could belong to wild animals or something else.

I'm the only one to travel this path on wheels, though, which means it will be easy to find our way back if we get lost. I have the flashlight rigged to sit on my head in a kind of headband I made by tying my socks together. It works like a coal miner's headlamp, lighting the trail in front of us while leaving my hands free to push my wheels. Sweaty feet are an acceptable sacrifice. Paul rides in my lap, holding the map so I can make sure we're still going the right way.

"I think we're close to the first *X*," he warns. I park my chair on the trail and examine the map. If my calculations are right, there should be a mine shaft around the next bend, somewhere off the trail and possibly swarming with demons. I grip Daddy's sword.

"What good is that thing gonna do?" Paul asks. "The note said you trap the demons in a ring of stones, then cast the charm—"

"Yeah, but I don't know what the charm *is*. Usually spells have special words. We're gonna have to improvise."

"I don't think *stabbing* things is a solution," Paul grumbles as I start pushing us forward again. "At least pick up some stones, will you? The one thing that actually *was* mentioned in that whole spiel?"

He has a point. I put the brakes on again and start looking around the trail for stones. I point to ones I like and Paul drags them over to me so I can fill the backpack.

The stones weigh down my chair, so it's a little harder to push once we start rolling again. Eventually I lean forward to balance the weight and get the hang of it.

As we near the bend, I push even slower. I round it slowly, shining the flashlight deep into the trees. I've never seen a demon before; who knows what I'm dealing with? "You sure this is where the *X* was? I don't see anything."

"Positive," Paul says, tapping the map in the darkness.

A sound comes from just off the trail—a high-pitched, shrieky chittering followed by something running through the underbrush. Paul and I both jump, the map flying up and landing on my hair. Paul scrambles up to my head, crouching on top of the flashlight where I can feel him quivering. That's when I see the "demon" on the trail: a large squirrel.

Paul slides back down my arm and lands in my lap, gesturing in the squirrel's direction. "*This* is what you were so dershrokn about?"

"You thought it was a demon, too," I grumble.

Paul ignores me. "Maybe these demons have moved on."

"Or maybe," I say, lifting my head to shine the light back into the woods, "somebody already hunted them."

Steering carefully, I venture off the trail and down into the trees where the *X*-marked shaft should be.

"You really think this is a good idea?" Paul asks. "Most people pass by a spot that's supposed to be full of demons and don't see any demons, they consider themselves lucky."

"But maybe Mama already caught them. There could be signs that'll help us find her." I pull back on my wheels as we roll into a very small clearing, then stop short. "Look," I whisper. Just beyond us—not more than thirty feet—is a rocky hill. There's a hole carved out of the side, maybe five or six feet tall and roughly shaped but propped up by wooden beams. Inside the opening, a wall of what looks like newly fallen rock blocks the tunnel. This is—or *was*— the first mine.

On the ground in front of the shaft, there's a circle of stones. A powderlike substance that looks like soot is spread from stone to stone.

"Kinda looks like a campfire," he says.

I shake my head. "There would still be wood, burned-out coals, *something*. And there would be ashes or coals *outside* the circle, too." I touch the ground outside the ring. "There's no ash out here, just dirt. And I've never seen a campfire where the ash inside made a perfect circle like that. This is something different. Something . . . not normal."

I reach into the circle and pinch some of the ash into my hand. It feels incredibly fine, almost silky, and doesn't leave any marks. It just slides between my fingers and drifts off into the air. What's left are dry, greenish-brown stubs.

"See?" Paul says. "There *was* wood on the fire!"

"This isn't wood," I say. "It's like, a weed or something. It's not even enough to use for kindling." I turn the bits over in my hand. They're not scorched. They remind me of . . . "Don't spells use herbs? Maybe that's what this is."

"Can you tell what kind?"

"No." I gather them into a little pile on a corner of the map and scoop up more ash, sifting that through my fingers, too. I do this until I have a small handful of the dried bits, hopefully enough to help if we do run into a demon. I stuff them into my pocket.

As we move on, I hear a snap behind me, like someone—or some*thing*—stepping on a twig. I whip my head around, but the forest is still and silent. *Another squirrel*, I tell myself.

"Hey, look," Paul says. He throws his weight against my cheek until my face turns in the direction he wants. The flashlight beam lands on another ring of stones a little farther off the trail. Just beyond it, I see another. There's a whole cluster of stone rings here, all filled with the same sootlike powder.

Then the light hits something else—a faint, iridescent glint a few yards ahead. Then, another glimmer closer to us. My eyes follow a trail that leads back to where we stand. Releasing my brakes and aiming the flashlight at the ground, I roll back. Mama's boot print. It was under me the whole time! And her prints point deeper into the woods.

"We gotta follow her tracks," I say.

"Do we, though?" Paul mutters, even though I'm already rolling us in that direction. "I mean, if these are demon traps, whatever demons were here must be gone now."

"But she might not be," I say.

We follow her tracks past the stone circles. The trees here grow close together, tall and thick. There's not much space to move between them—in places, it's barely wide enough for my chair. Ropelike roots clutter the surface and I have to pop last-minute wheelies over them, almost getting my casters caught more than once.

Occasionally, I catch glimpses of the moon through the branches. Here and there a faint glow seems to shimmer behind one of the trees, making me whip my head around. But mostly my flashlight is our only source of light. A fog has rolled in, too, making it hard to see more than a foot in front of my face.

Suddenly, my wheels hit something hard, not a root or a tree. It almost feels like . . . metal? I jerk to a stop, and the rocks in my backpack tip the back of my chair. Paul throws himself onto my feet to tip us forward, and I pull up on the brakes. We come to rest on my front casters with a force that knocks my teeth together.

I brush the dirt near my toes and feel something like a train rail, solid and made of steel. Here? In the woods?

I rear back and hop the rail, and maybe four feet across from it hit another. The tracks seem to start here, but where do they go? Rolling between the rails, I follow the tracks forward into the dark.

It's only a short distance before they disappear into the side of a hill, where another lumber-bracketed hole rises in front of us. I recall seeing pictures of mines with tracks running through them that were used for coal carts. This mine must be bigger than the last one; it gapes open into an even larger span of darkness.

I roll myself to the entrance and shine my flashlight around. At first I see only earthen walls and those rusty rails on the ground. As I wheel farther, though, the light catches something shiny, and I realize the ground is lined with objects: watches, keychains, and metal bottlecaps. Far off in the corner, I see the glinting dome of a metal hard hat, the kind loggers wear.

"Look at all this." I gasp. "I wonder where these people are now."

I feel a shiver move through Paul. I'm scared, too, but I reach down into the pile anyway. My hand scoops up a chain tangled in an old set of keys. My heart stops when I see what it is: a familiar-looking pendant.

"This is Millie Dobbs's necklace." I'm sure of it. That distinctive glow. That heart shape. Then another familiar glint of gold and ruby winks at me. Mama's earring.

I manage to launch out of my chair and snatch the earring, turning it over in my hands.

"Hey," Paul says softly. "Just because you found that doesn't mean she's not okay."

I close my hand around the earring and tuck it carefully into my pocket. He's right. She lost it before she even disappeared; maybe she never crossed paths with the demons. Still, the fact that they have something of hers doesn't exactly make me feel great. "I know. But just the thought . . . that something might have happened to her." I pause. "It's more important than ever that I find her, and fast."

I cram as much of the other stuff as I can into the backpack—just in case we track down their owners—and lay

Millie's pendant carefully on top. I'm rolling back out to the path when I hear a crackle.

The radio. Faraway music fading in and out of range, the same low, grumbling voices.

AND IT IS DONE?

"Yes, for now," says another voice.

Mama's voice.

SIXTEEN

I TURN UP THE VOLUME AS HIGH AS IT WILL GO, BUT IT DOESN'T get any louder.

YOU HAVE DONE WELL. THE GUARDIANS ARE IN YOUR DEBT.

Then the voices crackle and fade to dull static. I snatch the headphones and throw them across my knees.

"Guardians!" I say. "Get the map."

Paul drags it into my lap. "Look." I smooth out the wrinkles where the woods meet the mountains. "*Guardians.* She wrote it there."

"Okay . . . ?"

"And I heard them say it on the radio before. What does it mean?"

"Maybe something fighting the monsters?"

"Or maybe they *are* monsters! What if the demons work for them? Like, in monster movies, when there are little monsters there's usually a *big* monster, one that's even worse, leading them. And these things *sound* big."

"They don't sound angry, though. It sounds like she helped them."

"But what if she *had* to help them? What if they captured her and made her work for them?"

"Or maybe," Paul says somberly, "that's what her job *is*. Monsters or not, you have to help the people your job tells you to."

"No." I slam the map closed. "She wouldn't take a job like that."

"Perhaps you're right," he says in a gentle voice, patting my arm with the end of his tail. It's what he always does when he's trying to keep the peace between us, but I don't feel like being comforted right now. I jerk my arm away. "I'm just saying," he continues. "People make choices. Hard ones. Especially when they want what's best for the ones they love."

"What do you know?" I snap, giving him a hard look. "You're just something I made up."

Paul crawls up onto my armrest and wraps his tail around himself. I feel bad, but not sorry. Not yet.

I press the headphones to my ears, but the voices are gone. Now there's a cowboy song coming through, clear enough I can hear every word. No matter how I fiddle with the dial, I can't seem to get the voices back. We're far enough out of the trees to see the moon again, high above us and so pale it's almost blue. With the twang playing in my ears, I find where we left off and keep rolling on the trail.

We move in silence, punctuated only by forest sounds and the country radio. In the quiet, I think I hear another twig snap, another footfall I hope belongs to an animal. Finally, I break down. "How much farther to the next mine?"

"According to the map, it should be a little beyond that stand of trees." Paul points to a cluster of tall pines in the distance.

"Hey," I say. Paul has lowered his head to the map again. "I'm sorry about what I said. You can't help being a dragon. It doesn't mean you don't understand people."

"I appreciate that," he says with a deep nod. "But you know your mom better than I do. So if you say something about her, I should believe you."

"Thanks," I say. "Friends?" I extend my index finger to him.

He grabs it with both hands and shakes it. "Now both hands on the wheels before you run us into a ditch."

The trees on either side start to weave together. Their branches look like they're leaning in to whisper secrets. Without moonlight the path feels narrower, even though I can tell by looking at my wheel ruts that it's about the same. Again, I'm almost certain something behind the trees is glowing. But every glimpse moves too fast for me to be sure.

"Here," Paul says, and I hit the brakes.

"How do you know?"

Paul points off the trail, over a small drop into a thicket. I lean forward until I can see another stone ring. Another demon trap. Mama's boot treads move in the direction of the ring, and from there, deeper into the trees, then back out onto the trail.

I release the brakes and keep rolling.

"You're *not* going to check out the trap!"

"No," I agree. "But if we're going find Mama, we need to keep following her steps."

"Okay, then it looks like the next mine shaft is—!"

"What? Why did you—"

Then I'm tumbling forward, losing my grip on my chair as it loses its grip on the ground. And everything goes black.

SEVENTEEN

I OPEN MY EYES AND SEE FIRE. IT'S SO BRIGHT AFTER THE PITCH-dark that for a moment I think the forest is burning.

Then it all comes back. How I hit the ground on my stomach, dirt flying into my mouth and nose. How my chair slid out from under me. I don't know what happened to the map, or the flashlight, or my dad's sword.

Or to Paul.

I don't remember hitting my head, but it hurts. I try to reach a hand up to rub it, but my arm won't move.

Here's the thing about my kind of disability, though. Sometimes my arms and legs won't move the way I want them to, or when I want them to. It's like the signals don't make it from my brain to my body fast enough. When that happens, I just have to wait. Except having to wait for your limbs to figure out that your brain is telling them to move is kind of scary when you might be in the middle of a forest fire.

I try again to lift my hand and realize my arm won't move because it's *tied down*.

I pull harder, trying not to panic. The thought crosses my mind that I'm actually *in* the fire, like people being burned at the stake in movies. I don't feel like I'm burning, though; I just feel groggy.

As my eyes adjust, I can tell that the fire is several feet away. I'm also able to tell, mostly by feel, that it's not a stake I'm tied to. It's a massive rock.

Perched sentry-like around the fire, as if I've interrupted a clandestine meeting, are shadowy figures about the height of a medium-sized dog. The demons. And they've caught me.

In the flickering light, I realize they aren't just cloaked in shadows—they're made of shadows, at least partly. They're solid in the center, obsidian dark and ugly as gargoyles: some elongated and spiky, some squat as toads. Some have twisted horns sprouting from their heads or snaky tails whipping the air behind them or even shriveled, bat-like wings. Their shapes billow into the air around them, wispy enough to almost see through at the edges.

I hear their voices—high-pitched, nasal, and giggly— but I can't make out words. They sound nothing like the growls from the night radio station.

I try to wrestle against the ropes, which seem to be woven from some kind of thick vine.

But thrashing will only draw their attention. So I stay calm and press my back against the rock, wiggling my wrists against the ropes to loosen them.

I can't help but wonder if someone without my coordination problems could do a better job. But I snap myself out of those thoughts. *These are the only hands you've got. So you're going to have to work with them.*

I roll one of my wrists back and as I do, the rope around it starts to gap. The way my muscles work, I have to do everything backward. It's easier for me to pull than push. But the demons counted on me moving my hands the opposite way, the way most people's move. So instead of trapping myself tighter, I'm exposing a bubble in the rope.

I slip my hand out as slowly as I can. Soon both hands are free. But before I can escape, I have to figure out what they've done with my chair. Crawling through the forest doesn't seem like a workable idea, but maybe I can at least find a hiding spot.

That's when I hear a hiss from behind me. "Jerry!"

I turn to see something bluish and otherworldly behind a tree. Then the ghost of Chapel Bell steps toward me.

EIGHTEEN

CHAPEL IS GLOWING FROM HEAD TO TOE. HER DARK BROWN SKIN has a bluish tint, like the light is coming from somewhere inside her.

"What happened?" I whisper. I realize I'm about to cry. "Did the demons get you? Or—" I have a worse thought. "Was it the Guardians?"

Chapel squints. "What are you talking about?"

"The demons. The shadow monsters." I point to the fire, where they still sit, watching. But they're looking in the wrong direction, facing the path instead of the woods.

Her face lights up. "I know!" she says. "I mean . . ." She frowns at the ropes I've just freed myself from. "It's not cool that they caught you. But real monsters! Right here in Windy Pines."

"But didn't they catch you?" I ask. "Is that how you died?"

Confusion returns to Chapel's face. "And I ask you

again, *what* are you talking about?" she says.

Suddenly I remember stories about ghosts who don't know they're dead—who wander around the places they lived, doing the same things they did when they were alive. "You're a ghost," I say, as gently as possible. "You're dead."

Chapel laughs, then quickly claps a glowing hand over her mouth. She cuts her eyes over to the demons to make sure they didn't hear. "I'm not dead," she hisses. "Why on earth would you think I'm a ghost?"

I point at her other hand. "You're *glowing!*"

"This?" She lifts her hand and shakes it in front of my face. "It's just my dad's glow-in-the-dark stuff. It's like a lotion. You use it when you go camping so you can see in the dark."

I breathe a sigh of relief. "But . . . how are you *here?*"

"I'll explain later," she says. "First, we have to escape."

I take a quick look around. "Did you find my chair?"

"Yeah. But I couldn't bring it over without too much commotion. I hid it in a safe place."

"Wait. It's close?"

She nods.

"Okay. Can you get the backpack? If it's still there." I think of the pile of human things we found in the mine shaft. They might have all *my* things stashed away somewhere, too.

Chapel takes off, then returns a few minutes later,

weighed down by my bag. "Oof," she says as she swings it off her shoulders. "What's *in* this thing, rocks?"

"Actually, yes." I start placing the stones on the ground. "I read that you can trap a demon in a circle of stones. Since they all seem to be gathered around the fire, I *think* I have enough here to circle it and catch them. But we have to be *fast*."

Chapel frowns. "But won't they see us?"

Quietly as I can, I start crawling toward the demons. "Not if we keep silent and make the circle big enough to escape their notice. I can't have demons chasing me through the woods. This is the only way I can think of to stop them."

"Okay. I trust you."

We build as much of the circle as possible—maybe a quarter of an arc. Then I crawl to one end and lay down more, building it farther out. Chapel grabs the bag and runs in the other direction, dropping the stones into place as she goes.

We're a little less than halfway done when something chunks into the dust next to us. At first I think it's a stone, until another one strikes a nearby rock and splits it in half. I realize it's an awl, a metal wedge used to split wood. I glance in the direction it came from and see that the demons have spotted us.

They're barely ten yards away. I count at least eight, but

the shifting shadows could be hiding more. Their bodies seem to stretch and twist, claws and teeth bared, eyes glowing like coals in the darkness. Four of them shout and scramble toward us. I can't understand what they're saying, but their voices are like nails on a chalkboard.

Chapel hits the ground and rolls like a soldier in a movie, landing on her knees and pushing herself to her feet. She zips up the backpack and shifts it onto her shoulders, then takes off running into the trees. Great. The wheelchair kid gets left behind again.

If this *were* a movie, I would miraculously stand up and walk, cured by sheer determination and adrenaline. Instead, my legs feel even more weak and noodly than usual, so I crawl on my stomach as fast as I can. I know I can't outpace them, so instead I try to stay under their radar, slithering through the underbrush and pressing myself low to the ground, but I won't be able to evade them for long. I pick up a random rock and chuck it at them. It hits one square in the stomach, making it stagger. I grab another and bean a demon on the head.

Suddenly Chapel comes running out of the trees with my empty chair, which, except for a few scratches, looks fine. I crawl into the seat as fast as I can while Chapel grabs the loose ends of the rope the demons used to tie me and loops it several times around her waist, tying it off in a fancy knots. She doesn't even wait until my feet are settled on the footrests before pushing me out of the demons' grasp.

As we run into the woods, the trees begin to knit closer together until there's barely room to squeeze between them. Soon we stumble across a trail, not the main path but a crooked cow path, maybe an offshoot. The trees have spared it, leaning into each other instead of over the trail, and the red dirt seems to glow in the darkness, beckoning to us.

"When we get to a clearing, hit the brakes," she says in my ear. "I have an idea."

I skid to a stop near a small break in the trees. Tripping over one another has slowed the demons down, but they're still behind us, probably less than fifty yards away and gaining. Chapel unties the rope from her waist. "All-county double Dutch champion three years running," she says with a grin.

She ties one end of the rope to my handles and grips my shoulder. "When I say 'Go,' *go.*"

I nod. Now all the demons—at least a dozen—have escaped the broken circle and are heading our way en masse. Chapel waits until they've almost reached the tree line before whispering, "Go!"

I'm not really sure where I'm going, but I twist my waist to make my wheels wind from side to side as we weave between the trees.

"Yes!" Chapel cheers from behind me. She's running sideways in my wake, whipping the rope at the demons' heels. I look back to see them trip and stumble, falling and crashing into one another. The rope isn't enough to stop them, but at least it slows them down.

We crest over a rise and Chapel signals me to stop as she ties her end of the rope around a tree trunk. I understand what I have to do.

I circle an adjacent tree in my chair, wrapping the rope around its trunk. Now there's a taut wire like a clothesline stretched over the path. I unhook the rope from my chair handle and throw it to Chapel, who jumps up and loops it higher around the tree on her side before passing it back to me. A few more times around both trees and we've made a web, too tight for them to run through but hopefully hidden by the dip in the hill until it's too late.

Chapel slips the end of the rope off my handle, knotting it to my tree as I wedge a tall, leafy branch horizontally into the gap between our web and the tree next to it, blocking the path. Then we take off as fast as we can.

The demons shriek as they're snagged in our trap, and Chapel and I coast down the other side of the hill. When we reach the bottom, I look back and see the rest of them going around the pileup or clawing their way up the neighboring trees and vaulting off onto the slope.

We have a head start, though. In the dark, the demons' shadowy forms blur into the night, but we can see their glowing red eyes and hear the scratchy footfalls of their long-clawed feet. When those fade far enough into the background for me to hope they can't see us, I signal to Chapel and we veer right into a dense stand of trees.

We break through a thicket and back onto the main path, pausing to catch our breath and pick burrs and thorns from our clothes and hair. Without the light of the fire, the darkness of the forest has swallowed us. Chapel pulls out her cell phone and hits the flashlight button.

"Your parents let you have a phone?" I blurt. Maybe a weird question right now, but I can't help it.

"My parents have rules about how much I can use it. But I'm not even supposed to be out here right now. I'm gonna get in trouble anyway."

"At least you have one. I'm not allowed." In my head, I can hear Paul's voice every time Mama turned me down when I asked for my own phone. *Who would you call, anyway?* Maybe I'd call Chapel. If we ever make it out of here.

"It doesn't have a signal. But at least it has a light!"

Chapel's phone light doesn't cover as much ground as my flashlight did, but it's enough to illuminate a slab of wood too straight and square to be a tree trunk.

"Chapel," I whisper. "Shine it over there."

Once she does, I can make out the weathered support beams of another mine shaft.

She shines her light on the entrance while I ease off my brakes and duck my head to roll inside. The opening is low and narrow; as soon as I cross the threshold, the floor drops out from under me. I hit the lowered walkway with a tooth-chattering *thud*. It takes a moment, but my bones settle and my eyes adjust to the dark. I notice stashes of shiny things tucked into the corners around the beams: the same mix of jewelry, accessories, and trash as before.

The faint hum of static leads me to my radio and headphones. I find the radio's plastic body by feel. The flashlight is nearby, but not the map. There's also a (probably long-dead) phone and a wallet with a silver chain. A bracelet with a heart charm. A set of keys with a rhinestone-studded bottle opener on the keyring. I scoop all of it up.

My flashlight beam bounces off a long streak of silver, and tears jump into my eyes as I recognize Daddy's sword.

I carefully pull it out and lay it across my knees, using my shirt to wipe away dirt and soot until I can see my face reflected in the metal again. Then there's the scrabble of feet. My eyes widen as Paul darts out of the nest.

You're okay! I mouth to him. He ducks into a sweeping bow before climbing into my jacket pocket. Something relaxes through my whole body as I feel him curl up against my hip. I turn to look at Chapel—now that Paul can move objects in this spooky forest, who knows if others can see him?—but she's turned away, rooting through the rest of the loot.

A moment later, her voice rings out. "You're jealous of me for having a phone, but you have a *sword*?"

NINETEEN

"SO HOW *DID* YOU FIND ME OUT HERE?" I ASK.

We continue on the path in search of Mama. I pause every now and then to pick up a new arsenal of stones. Even without the map, it hasn't been hard to find our way—the trail is fairly well-worn. But we don't know where the nests are, so we have to stay alert.

"I saw you on my way home from dance practice," Chapel says. "Going into the woods. I figured you had a good reason. But the woods aren't safe and I didn't want you to go alone. So I ran back to my room and got my wilderness stuff and came after you. You weren't hard to find. I followed your tire tracks in the mud."

I look behind me at the twin ruts furrowing through the ground. It's so strange to think that while I was following Mama's boot prints, Chapel was following *me*. I recall the glow of light behind us, the times I thought I heard something nearby, and feel relief, if only for a second. "But weren't you scared?"

She rubs her glittery arms. "Sure. But I've been reading about wilderness survival. I thought maybe I could be a rescuer someday."

"I thought you wanted to be a ghost."

"I have to be something *before* that, though! I told you I want to live a long time."

"Future ghost, jump rope champion, dancer, wilderness rescuer . . ." I tick them off on my fingers.

"I was in the Brownies until I got kicked out for trying to bring home a squirrel from camp."

I can't stifle my laugh. "What?"

"Well, it wasn't so much the squirrel itself, even though they *were* mad about that. It was just a baby and I was trying to help. I got kicked out because the squirrel escaped in the back of the van and chewed through two tents and five boxes of cookies." She shrugs wistfully. "But I *did* learn some wilderness survival skills on that trip."

I think about Chapel going into the woods to save people. She'd be good at it. "You already rescued me," I say. "So you've got a head start!"

"I mean, I hope I did," she says. "We're still in the woods with demons after us."

I scan the rows of knotty pines with my headlamp. There's a quick flash of something—a long, white skull with antlers, like a deer, standing tall on two legs. It runs off into the trees and disappears.

I grip Chapel's forearm. "Did you see that?"

"See what?"

Suddenly I'm not sure I saw it, either. *My eyes are playing tricks on me*, I think.

We're quiet for a moment, focused on finding stones and watching the trail. "You know the map I had?" I say. I had already told her about the map, the *X*s that marked demon nests, and how I'd been tracking Mama.

"Yeah."

"It also said that these roads lead to something called Guardians. I've heard that term before. Sometimes at night the radio picks up this strange station. I know it sounds really weird, but I hear voices talking about Guardians over the radio."

"Do you know what they are?"

"No. But I think they're monsters. Like, maybe they're the final-boss monsters. And my mama . . ." I swallow. "My mama's *helping* them for some reason. I don't know if they're *forcing* her. But I don't think she's safe."

I hold up the radio. "Maybe we can find them with this. The signal cuts in and out. But if we pick up the station again, we might be able to figure out where it's coming from."

"And hey, at least now we know what a demon looks like!" she says. She adds another rock to the bag and zips it back up. "I think that's all that'll fit!"

"Awesome. Thanks!"

Chapel shifts her pace so she's walking next to me, almost skipping really. The path is just wide enough for the two of us, and her arm brushes against mine as I reach for my wheels. Every time it does, I get a little jolt of electricity that seems to make my heart beat one notch faster. I don't think I have a crush on Chapel, exactly. It's more than that. Knowing her has changed everything, but at the same time, I feel like I've known her all my life.

"So why don't you go to my school, *really*?" she asks after we've been moving for a while.

It's the first thing she's said tonight that isn't about demons or ghosts or maps or swords. And since I can't be sure we'll make it out of here alive, the usual *I'm home-schooled* doesn't seem like enough. It feels like I could tell her everything and it wouldn't matter. Like when this is all over—if this is *ever* over—what I say now won't count.

So I take a deep breath and tell her the truth.

"I used to go to school," I tell her. "A couple of different schools, actually. In a couple of different towns. We traveled a lot after my dad died. But everybody was too mean. So I just . . . stopped going."

"You *dropped out*?"

"I didn't drop out! I just learn in other ways. Like, I read a lot. And I was supposed to start getting these packets from the school district that would make me an official homeschool student, once we were settled, but now . . ." My voice cracks.

Chapel puts her hand on my arm on purpose this time. I stop pushing my wheels. "Hey," she says. "We're gonna find her, okay?"

I nod, wiping my nose on the sleeve of my jacket. "Okay."

She leans over and wraps me into a hug. My whole body relaxes and my breathing becomes steadier. It really does feel, in this moment, like everything *is* gonna be all right.

I realize I haven't hugged anyone besides Mama in while, maybe not since Daddy's been gone. For so long it's felt like everyone has either hated me or pitied me; I can't recall the last time I trusted someone enough to let them get this close. But Chapel's arms wrapped around me feel warm and solid. Safe.

We stay like this for a while. When she lets go, I notice that some of the sparkly stuff has smeared onto the front of my jacket, and now I have a ghostly glow of my own. I smile at the idea that some of her shine has rubbed off on me.

Then there's crackle in my headphones. *UNREST IN THE FOREST TONIGHT. THE TREES SPEAK OF UNFINISHED WORK.*

Chapel's eyes widen. "Are those the voices? What does *that* mean?"

I nod. "I don't know. But the signal is getting clearer. We must be headed in the right direction."

"The right direction for what?"

"To find . . . *it*. Whatever *it* is, it has my mama." I pause. "It's okay if you want to turn around, go back home."

"I'm not gonna leave you alone here."

I smile.

We keep moving until the moon breaking through the trees illuminates a drop-off ahead. As we get closer, I notice a steep downhill turn.

"Do you trust me?" I ask Chapel.

"Of course," she says.

"See the pegs on the back of my chair? Grab my push handles and climb onto those pegs. And then hold on *tight*."

When she does, I roll us to the edge, grasp my sword, and let the wheels go.

And we fly.

TWENTY

"HANG ON!" I YELL AS WE RATTLE DOWN THE TEETH-CHATTERING drop. Rocks clatter down the slope as we pick up speed, and it creates a kind of rhythm with the clacking of the beads at the ends of Chapel's braids.

Gradually the road starts to even out, but the dirt at the bottom is fine and thick, like sand. It shifts under my wheels, pulling them into a tilting zigzag from side to side. "We're tipping!" I yell.

My chair careens to one side, so I throw my weight against the opposite armrest. Behind me, Chapel throws both feet onto the far peg and leans hard. The chair straightens and we coast through the sandy dirt until it's hard and flat enough for me to pull up on the brakes, and we skid to a stop.

As the dust settles, Chapel hops off and holds up her hand for a high five. I lift my hand, still wobbling from the rough ride, and slap her palm.

"Better than a roller coaster," she says with a shaky grin.

I smile, then grip my wheels, ready to roll on, when the sound of talons on stony earth makes me freeze. A shadow crosses our path. Before I can react, a demon pops out of the trees and grabs my arm, digging its claws into my flesh. I cry out, and it smiles. A tingle ripples up my skin, a stinging shimmer that moves and dances.

"Jerry!" Chapel grabs my sword and swings it at the demon. It shrieks as the blade slashes its arm, and a dark, purplish substance oozes to the surface. It bubbles like it's boiling, steam rising around the wound. And then, just as quickly, the skin closes up again.

The demon's touch is like an electric shock that rushes through me. I'm sliding down in my chair as a warmth in my muscles make them feel like noodles.

I try to fight it, but it's like trying to swim against a current. My eyes close for a second, and it feels so peaceful. I could give in to this. I could let it happen. It would be so nice. . . .

"JERRY!"

Chapel's shriek snaps my eyes open. I dig my nails into my armrests, pull myself up as much as I can, and blink. "I—I can't . . . stay . . . awake."

"They're confusing you," she says. "We read about this, remember? It's their magic. You have to fight it!"

Then she swings the blunt end of the sword wildly and

hits the demon again. It staggers, its long, crabby fingers unwinding from my arm, and suddenly it's easier to sit up. There's still a buzzing in my bones, but my body slowly begins to feel like my own again.

The demon lunges at Chapel, knocking her back. She catches herself before she falls, but not before it grabs her ankle. The air around her shimmers, then her eyes roll back in her head, and she collapses.

Now that I can move my limbs, I manage to grab the sword, which had fallen to the ground. Instead of using it, though, I unzip my backpack and stones clatter to the ground.

The demon jumps and spins to face me. I turn my chair around as fast as I can, kicking the rocks into a circle with my feet. The demon grabs a thin branch and lunges toward me, jamming it through the spokes of one of my wheels.

I spin back, my stuck wheel grinding in place while the other one swings in a half circle and kicks up dust. I'm too panicked for my hand to grasp the stick. My fingers flutter like useless moths.

Before I can open my mouth to yell or scream, I feel a rustle on my chest. Paul slithers out of my pocket and takes a leap, hopping off the armrest of my chair and landing on the branch. It bends and bounces under his weight but stays firmly lodged in my spokes. He jumps again, landing harder this time, and I hear a crack.

Then I freeze. The demon has grabbed on to my wheel and is trying to climb up my chair. It's so close to Paul. It reaches out its spindly fingers. . . .

Paul jumps again and the wood splits. In the smoothest move I've ever seen, he leaps back onto my armrest, snatching half of the stick out of midair while the other half clatters to the ground.

Then Paul *fights* the demon, swinging his stick and catching it across the throat. The demon falls back, gasping. Quick as I can, I shove the last stones into place. The ring I've made isn't going to win any art contests, but it's roughly a circle, and it surrounds the demon on all sides. I can only hope that's enough.

The demon tries to leap forward as I roll away, but it can't cross the circle. I turn toward Chapel, but she's not there.

"Chapel!" There's a muffled shout up ahead, then I notice scuffs in the dirt, two deep grooves. I grab my wheels and follow them until I see the demons dragging her through the woods.

By the time I catch up, they've noticed me. Two of them jump up and fly through the air, landing on the back of my chair. Their electric talons latch onto my shoulder, and warm waves wash over me again, threatening to pull me under.

I summon all the strength within to slash at them with

my sword. The blade slices into the shoulder of the one holding Chapel. It hisses and jumps back, and the others back away, leaving Chapel on the ground. I rock my chair hard to the side, knocking off the hitchhikers. Then I use the sword to frantically saw at the ropes binding her hands. The vines finally split in the middle and slither to the ground like snakes.

"Chapel! Wake up!" I'm still holding the sword in front of us, fending off our would-be attackers.

She blinks her deep brown eyes, staring like she doesn't know who I am. Then the clouds roll away from her face.

"Are you okay?" I ask.

"I—I think so."

I help her steady her arms while she pulls herself to her feet. "I don't know if there are more around. But my wheels should give us an advantage. Hop on!"

Chapel grabs a few rocks that fell out in the struggle and zips them back into the backpack. She puts her feet on the pegs and grabs hold of my handles. Then I push off.

We careen around the side of a tree, so close to it that I flinch. I grip my handlebar seconds before a demon's claws gouge into the bark. The sounds of falling rocks and snapping twigs echo behind us. They're in hot pursuit and gaining on us.

With a *thud* that shakes the ground, something drops from above and lands in front of us. I screech to a halt seconds before we collide with a pair of glowing eyes. A demon hand reaches toward us but only swipes my wheel.

That's when Chapel seems to come fully awake. She takes control, swiveling my chair hard and zipping us out of its grasp.

We're zooming down a narrower side trail now, the skittering behind us growing fainter, but I can't shake the feeling we're not alone.

"Chapel," I whisper. "Look up." Our eyes follow the tree trunks up to their branches, where dozens of eyes gleam in the dark, claws scraping the bark as their owners shift their weight, ready to pounce.

Chapel leans over the back of my chair to whisper in my ear. "Do you trust me?" Her breath tickles the back of my neck.

I nod.

"They go up, we go down!" she yells.

We take off rolling down a steep embankment on the side of the trail. I see the dark shimmer of water just before we fall into it.

The water is almost waist high on Chapel and it sloshes over my seat. Slimy tendrils of something brush against my skin. It's not easy to push through the silty sludge on the bottom, and my shoulders ache by the time we're rolling up the slope on the other side.

We've lost the trail completely, but at least there's no

sign of demons over here.

"Survival trick," Chapel says through her pants for air. "Works for dogs, I figured why not try it with demons?"

"Dogs can't cross water?"

"I mean, some can, but going through water throws them off your scent. Which will at least slow them down!"

We find a gap behind two boulders where the hill dips in like a shallow cave. Chapel pushes me inside and we squash ourselves against the wall until we hear splashing, footfalls, shouts through the trees, and finally . . . silence. We exhale at the same time, but we wait a little longer, until we're sure the demons ran a different way.

"Let's go." I reach for Chapel's hand. That's when I notice she's frozen against the wall, her eyes wide and barely blinking. "What is it? What's wrong?"

Chapel gulps so hard I can see the air caught in her throat. I follow the line of her eyes to the overhanging corner of our little alcove, where a nest of small brown spiders sways gently on a silky web. "Are you afraid of spiders?"

Chapel nods. It's strange to her trembling. I thought she was completely fearless.

"I've got this." I squeeze her hand. It's my turn to be brave. "I'll go first, okay? I'll get in between."

Chapel bites her lower lip and nods.

I roll to her other side and plant myself between her and the web. Strands of spider silk brush against my shoulders but I don't flinch. I squeeze Chapel's hand one more time and she takes a deep breath, stepping past me and the spiders back into the woods.

Outside the cave and around the hill, we roll into a clearing, a meadow with blue-green grasses swaying in the wind. It's quieter, and the full moon shines clear above us, the most light we've seen in a long time. The mountains still loom in the distance, dark swirls of fog clinging to their rocky faces, but even they can't blot out the light. I park my chair and Chapel sits down beside me.

"My parents are probably out searching for me," she says. "If we survive this, I'm gonna be grounded till I'm thirty."

"At least they care enough to worry."

"Oh. I'm sorry—"

"I mean—I didn't mean my mama doesn't care. I know she does! If she's still . . ." I shake my head. "Just I'm glad you have them, you know? I'm glad you have someone to worry."

"It's weird for our family," she says. "Living together in that room. We trip over one another; we get on one another's nerves." She laughs. "But now, they always know right away when something's wrong. Sometimes they know before *I* do."

"I get it," I say softly. "Ever since it's been just me and

Mama, we've been closer than other people seem to think is normal. We talk about stuff other kids don't talk about with their parents. She doesn't treat me like I'm a kid who won't understand."

I take a deep breath. "That's why this has been so hard. She's been keeping all kinds of secrets from me. I didn't know she was hunting demons. I didn't even know she *knew* about the Guardians, and all this time she's been *working* with them!"

"She was probably trying to protect you," Chapel says.

"I guess. But she's always trusted me with the truth. Even when Daddy died. She told me exactly what happened, she let me come to the funeral, she treated me like I was a real person who was hurting, too." I wipe my eyes. "If she's keeping all these secrets now, what does that mean about before? Were there more secrets I didn't know about?"

"Your mama's the only one who knows for sure. And when we find her, you'll ask."

I nod. "You know, you're the first person I've met in a while who's treated me like I'm . . . normal. You don't pretend my chair isn't there, but you don't act like it makes me weird or that I can't do anything." I think about Miss Mavis and some of my teachers. "Even adults don't get it right most of the time. Everybody either feels sorry for me, or they make fun of me, or they try to act like I'm not different, but since I *am* different and it's not always something they can ignore, they just end up ignoring *me*."

"In a different kind of way, I get it," Chapel says. "I've lived in Windy Pines since I was in third grade and it's pretty diverse here, but where I lived before, I was one of the only Black kids in my school. Almost everybody else was white. And most of the people there weren't exactly *mean* about it. They just had this idea that treating me like I was exactly the same as them was like treating me as their equal. I mean, they would actually pretend they didn't notice that I'm different. Even little things—like at sleepovers when I'd wrap my hair before bed. Or like, when we'd dress up and do makeovers, their makeup colors were wrong for me, and nobody wanted to admit that my skin tone was different, that my hair was different. And the girls in the magazines we looked at usually didn't look like me, but they wouldn't *talk* about that. I think they thought they were showing they accepted me by pretending there weren't any differences between me and the white models with the straight blonde hair, but if they'd actually talked to me, they'd know I don't *want* to look like them. I *like* looking like me." She sighs. "And they had this way of congratulating themselves for it. Like it made them good people to not see me for who I am. It just got really exhausting."

I wipe my face one more time. The rough denim feels good, like it's scrubbing away some of the fear. "That must have been hard." At least when people can't see my chair, they don't know I'm different. Chapel doesn't have that luxury.

"It was. But I found real friends eventually. And I dunno." She shrugs. "I guess you kind of see people better when you're used to not being seen. I had to learn that in order to figure out who really liked me for me."

"I like you for you," I say. "It means a lot that you gave me a chance to. After the way those other kids treated you, I'd understand why you wouldn't trust me." My stomach wobbles. "Can I tell you something else?"

"Sure."

"I was afraid to be your friend. I thought you'd leave and then it would be worse than if I hadn't gotten to know you at all. I'm sorry I didn't trust you more."

"But . . ." She smiles. "We're friends now, right?"

"Definitely." I smile back.

The radio crackles, and I hear the voices again, though I can't make out what they're saying. I move it until the signal comes in more clearly and roll a short distance away. It stays strong. "This way. We need to follow the signal."

Just then, I feel tiny, clawed feet climbing from my chest

to my shoulder.

"Pfft!" Paul takes a deep breath. "I couldn't stay in there any longer! You know how hard it is to breathe?"

I rub the top of his head with one finger, a small enough gesture that Chapel might not even notice.

But instead she cries, "Jerry! There's a . . . dragon on your shoulder!"

TWENTY-ONE

MY JAW DROPS. "YOU CAN *SEE* HIM?"

She squints. "What is it? A toy? It looks so real!"

I shake my head. "Not at all. I mean, he's always been real to me. But other people usually can't see him." Paul climbs into my open palm, and I lift him to Chapel's eye level. "This is Paul."

She shakes her head in disbelief, then reaches toward him. "*Is* he a dragon? Dragons are real, too?"

Paul crosses his arms. "*He* can talk, ya know!"

"Paul!" I snap. "She didn't know that!"

"Sorry," he grumbles.

"I'm sorry, too," says Chapel. "I've never met a dragon before." She shakes her head groggily.

"Eh, there's all kinds of dragons. Like there's all kinds of people. You meet one, doesn't mean you met 'em all." He pulls himself back up to his full height and extends his hand. "Name's Paul."

Chapel's eyes are huge as she grasps Paul's hand between her thumb and forefinger and gives it a light shake. "I'm . . . Chapel."

"Nice to meet ya." Paul scurries back up to my shoulder.

"I'm sorry I didn't tell you about him before," I say. "I honestly didn't think anybody but me could see him."

"So, you thought he was, like, an imaginary friend?"

I duck my head. It still feels so babyish to hear that. "Yeah, kind of. I mean, I didn't really have a lot of friends. So I thought I made one up." I wait for her to laugh.

Instead, she nods. "That makes sense."

"It does?"

"Yeah. You know I love ghost stories, right? Well, I used to pretend to see ghosts sometimes. Pretend I could talk to them and nobody else could. Like, ghosts of people who were young and cool and would understand me better than people my age who are alive."

"But . . . you grew out of it, right?"

"I wouldn't say that. Things just got better for me, and then I didn't need to do it anymore. It wasn't so much about growing up as about finding my place." She sets her hand on the shoulder Paul isn't sitting on. "Anyway, I don't judge you for needing a friend, or for finding a dragon! But I can see him. And I think he's cool."

On my shoulder, Paul shakes his scales off like a wet cat. "So, no more hiding in that musty old pocket, huh?"

he says. "Like a cave in there." He goes on muttering to himself, half in English and half in Yiddish.

"Just ignore him," I whisper.

"I heard that." Paul snorts and curls into a ball on my shoulder.

I turn my attention to the meadow. The tall grass has been flattened in areas, letting us know someone was here. Without a map or a trail, my only guide is the radio station. Right now I hear only static and a low rumbling, but this was the last place I heard Mama's voice, so I have to believe it will lead me to her. It's the only thing I have left to go on.

The grass gets thinner and lower as we reach the edge of the clearing, then it gives way to moss and lichen, a more compact surface that feels like Miss Mavis's living room carpet. It's easier than rolling through the grass, which was like trying to move underwater. Now I don't need Chapel's help to push my chair.

Soon the darkness of the woods closes around us and the ground becomes hard-packed dirt. I jump in my seat as I catch a glimpse of something with long, scraggly hair draped over a short body with long arms. It's there and gone like a film frame so I can't be sure I really saw it. When I scan the trees again and find nothing, I release my breath.

Eventually we pick up the path again, and my wheels

press their twin ruts into the soil, marking our trail. And just as the flashlight beam becomes our only line of sight, I see its glow bounce off an oily boot print.

"Look!" I shout. "I *knew* she came this way!"

Chapel bends down and throws her arms around me. "We're gonna find her. I can feel it."

"Thank you," I whisper, squeezing back.

She holds up her cell phone light to help illuminate our path. The radio station is still fading in and out, but the signal seems to be getting stronger.

Just as I'm celebrating having the footprint trail back, it disappears again. I pull back on my wheels and jerk to a stop.

"Look!" Paul says. He slides down to my knee and points off the path. There's a print a few feet down the fairly steep embankment. Did she jump? Or fall?

I shake off the thought and roll myself to the edge. The ground is rough and uneven, full of rocks and tree roots. They reach out like sinister fingers, waiting to grab my wheels and pull me down.

"Jerry." Chapel tugs on my sleeve and I follow her eyes to a familiar-looking, ash-filled rock ring. A few feet away there's another . . . and another. There must have been demons here. Maybe another mine shaft nearby, but I don't see anything, and without the map I have no guide. If there *were* demons, it looks like Mama got to them first.

I feel a little bit proud and a lot scared at the same time.

"I don't get it." I move my head to drag the flashlight across the rough ground and back onto the path. "Her footprints go off the trail, but they don't come back."

"Maybe there's another trail down there." Chapel scans the ground with her phone.

"It doesn't look like it. The brush is too thick to get very far."

From where I sit, it really looks like she just jumped off the trail to set the traps and then her tracks disappeared.

The speakers crackle just before the music is drowned out by a horrible, loud screech, like a train dragging to a stop. The sound of something laughing in the background—*cackling*—feels like a scrape against my bones.

Then I'm blinded by a flash. The ground shifts under my wheels like an earthquake, and I can feel myself tipping. I clutch the sides of my chair as it careens sideways and tumbles end over end with me inside it. My wheels lift off the ground before I come slamming back down on my side, chair and all.

A shadow streaks away into the night, too dark and fast to see, but more screechy cackles trail behind it.

As the dust settles, I push myself up on my elbow until I can crane my neck and see lights—not just firelight, but lamps, torches, strings of lanterns. There are ten or more nests clustered around the mouth of a cave straddled by flaming pine-pitch torches. My sideways position has me pinned to the ground, though I don't feel hurt. I don't see Chapel or Paul.

Shadows on the paths stretch into demons, two dozen at least, moving closer and closer in the dark mist. The ones in front crawl on all fours, slithering low with their haunches raised. Behind them, legions more lunge toward me on their hind legs, faces twisted into menacing grins.

I'm surrounded. There are too many of them to fight or trap. It feels as if all the demons in the woods are closing in on me at the same time.

I fumble to unbutton my chest pocket. The pearl button is shiny and round, and it glints in the moonlight. I have a hard time with buttons, even using both hands, but finally I manage to pop it off. It flies and bounces in the dirt, until the demon closest to me, one with a spiky tuft on its head, runs to snatch it, cradling it in its hand like a precious jewel.

I scoop the herbs out of my pocket and fling them into the crowd. They hit one demon in the eyes, stunning it and buying me a moment to think. That's when I notice the spike-headed demon still cackling over my pocket button.

I curl my fingers around Mama's earring. *She'll understand.* I pause for a second, feeling the fake jewels warm in my hand. The earring feels alive—like it's part of her. And somehow, that thought helps.

Just as a demon is about to grab me, I throw the earring as far as I can, tipping my head up so the headlamp catches the rhinestones and makes them sparkle.

It hits the ground several yards behind them with a puff of dust. Then the demons—even the one grabbing for me—run, stumbling and clambering over one another, and pile on the spot where the earring fell.

While they're distracted, I feel around the ground for the radio and sword, which luckily didn't fall too far. I tuck the radio into my pocket and brace the sword against the ground, pushing against it to tip my chair. I manage to lift the frame a few inches off the ground, then my strength gives out.

The backpack full of rocks! I reach behind me and wrestle with the straps, but they're twisted around my handles, weighing my backpack to the ground. I don't have the coordination to free them.

My flashlight glints on the blade of the sword. For the first time, I notice the initials engraved where the blade meets the hilt: JEB. My dad's initials—Joshua Eli Blum—but also mine. I know what my dad would do, what the heroes in his adventure stories would do. I can be a warrior, too.

I swing the blade over my shoulder and slash the canvas straps, first one and then the other. There's a *thud* as the sack of rocks hits the ground.

The demons hear it, too. Three of them untangle themselves from the pile and run in my direction, followed by a few more. I push off on the sword again with every bit of strength I've got. With a creak and a shudder, my chair flips back onto its wheels.

"Jerry!"

Behind me, a bruised and scraped Chapel rises from a ditch. Paul is perched on her shoulder as if he belongs there, and in spite of everything I feel a twitch of a smile.

Now the demons move in on us from all sides. Chapel grabs my backpack off the ground and tosses it into my lap, and I grip my handles as she starts running, pushing me deeper into the trees.

Paul hooks his claws into the fabric of Chapel's jacket, holding on as tight as he can. The demons are on our tail, but Chapel manages to stay a step ahead of them until we burst into a very small, mossy clearing surrounded by thick trees. Sitting in the middle of the clearing is a house.

TWENTY-TWO

IT'S A SMALL HOUSE, MORE OF A SHACK, REALLY, WITH GRAY boards covered in shakes and shingles that look beaten by years of sun and rain and time. Its wooden door is almost flat to the ground, with just a small gap that I easily pop a wheelie over.

Without thinking, I grab for the doorknob and Chapel jumps ahead to swing it open. It slams behind us just as the demons burst into the clearing. Chapel bolts the door with a heavy latch. As we catch our breath and look around, we realize we're trapped.

"What now?" Chapel whispers.

I pull back a musty curtain and peer out one of the thick, dirty windows. From what I can see, we're surrounded by demons, but they're hanging back by the tree line. They look like they're pressing against an invisible barrier, as if the house is wrapped in magical cling wrap that won't let them through.

"I don't think they can get in here."

"That doesn't make sense."

With the demons seemingly at bay, I let myself relax enough to take a look around. The house has dried plants and herbs hanging from bare rafters, and its walls are lined with cluttered shelves. A closer look reveals rows upon rows of jars; one looks like it's full of eyeballs; another is filled with something red that resembles a root.

I remember the voice on the radio: *the witch of the woods.* "Ummmm . . ."

Chapel turns around, gently setting down another jar that has what looks like a brain floating in it and wrinkling her nose. "Yeah?"

"I think we're in a witch's house."

"A *bad* witch?" Chapel bites her lower lip.

"I'm not sure." My eyes land on a narrow, army-style cot with sagging springs. A new-looking sleeping bag lies half unzipped on the mattress. "Someone's been here." I set my backpack on the floor and roll closer.

Next to the sleeping bag there's an empty water glass; an old-fashioned alarm clock, the kind you have to wind; and a framed picture. *My* picture. A photo from the last school I went to, my hair slicked back and my shirt buttoned uncomfortably high, an awkward smile against an ugly backdrop.

Who would leave my dorky picture next to their bed but Mama?

"Chapel!" I exclaim. "I think—"

"I found something!" she shouts back.

I roll across the room to a wooden countertop covered with pestles and mortars and various tools. Chapel is holding a yellowed piece of paper. Something about it clicks in the back of my head. I pull out the folded-up paper I found in Mama's car. The crabbed handwriting is identical.

"'Like every house I have a floor,'" she reads. "Is this supposed to be written by the house?" I shrug and she reads on. "'In the floor, there is a door.'"

"It's a poem!" I flap my own paper in the air. "The other half is here. It tells us how to fight the demons!"

"It sounds more like a riddle." Chapel scrunches her face. "In the floor there is a door?"

"Is there anything else?"

"'Use it only if you need, for to the beasts the path will lead.'"

"The beasts? That must mean the demons!"

Chapel twists a braid. "How do you know?"

I hold up my radio. "That station I was telling you about, the one that comes in late at night. The voices talk about terrible things in these woods: the beasts, the mines. We know the demons hide in the mines; it's probably them!"

"But why would the witch or whoever want to point

anyone *toward* the demons?"

I glance over at the rumpled bed. "To hunt them."

Chapel's eyes follow mine. "And you think if we find the demons, we'll find your mom."

I nod. "And with so many of them out *there*"—I point in the direction of the window—"maybe there aren't any wherever this leads." I point to the bottom half of the poem she's holding. "Or at least, not as many."

Chapel takes a deep breath. "Okay, then we need to figure this out." Her eyes flick down to the paper. "'In the floor, there is a door.'" She scans the ground for anything that looks like a door, but the broad floorboards, the same gray as the rest of the house, all look relatively even.

"Wait." I remember hearing a slight creak in the floor when I rolled from the bed. I roll back to the same spot and rock on my wheels, listening to the difference in the rumble of the boards under me. Something feels off in one spot, but I don't *see* anything different—no handles or knobs, not even a seam that doesn't match the others.

Chapel drops to her hands and knees, crawling around the same patch of floor. She presses her ear to the wood and knocks, once, twice, three times. On the third knock, a rectangle swings away underneath her as if it were loaded on a spring. She jumps back just in time to keep from falling into a dark hole the size of a bathtub.

"Door in the floor," Chapel whispers, crawling toward

the edge to peer down into the hole. I roll as close as I can. A set of rough wooden steps, maybe four or five, stretches down into the darkness. My flashlight reflects off cobwebs stretched across the bottom of the stairs; little jewels of water trapped in the threads catch the light. Chapel glances at the stairs and then back at me, a wrinkle crossing her forehead.

"I can deal." I grab my backpack off the floor, dump out the rest of the rocks, and tie the straps back together around my handles before setting my brakes and scooting out of my chair. I don't *like* doing this, but I can if I have to.

Stretching up to grab the handles of my chair, I tip it onto its back wheels while I swing my legs around to sit on the top step. *Bump, bump, bump, bump, bump.* One, two, three, four, five. I push the chair in front of me and scoot my butt down the stairs.

At the bottom, my feet hit a floor that feels like packed dirt. I flip my chair around and climb into it as Chapel comes down after me. She starts to close the trapdoor behind her, then seems to think better of it.

The room we're in feels like some kind of cellar, except that the ceilings are very low and the walls are close. Everything about it seems designed to push us forward, the only way we can go.

TWENTY-THREE

WE CAN SEE ONLY FIVE FEET AHEAD, EVEN WITH MY FLASHLIGHT guiding the way. It's clear now we're not in an ordinary cellar but a narrow passageway, a tunnel. Chapel bends over the back of my seat and even I dip my head reflexively.

Suddenly a shadow swoops in front of us. Chapel screams and I slam on my brakes.

Above us, more small, dark shapes huddle and tremble. "Bats," she says, shuddering. I exhale. Bats, I can deal with.

We coast down what feels like a ramp. The dirt is just firm enough to roll on without getting stuck but still loose enough to gum up my wheels. The walls smell like wet soil and worms.

It's a long descent underground, becoming darker the deeper we go. Finally, I feel the ground level out under my wheels.

It's hard to tell how long we're rolling; the darkness seems to swallow time. Just when the walls start crowding my shoulders, the tunnel widens again. There are lamps on either side of us, maybe old mine lamps? They're dark, but torches mounted on the walls give a little light. The torches aren't much higher than Chapel's waist, but in my chair they're not far below my eye level.

I stop. "These must be the demons' torches." I crane my neck to look for any signs of Mama.

"I'm going to investigate ahead," Chapel says.

"Okay. Don't go too far." I bend down and start searching the ground for clues, when I hear a scream.

"Chapel!" My heart pounds in my ears. A few yards ahead, she's sprawled on the ground with ropes around her legs. "Are you hurt?"

She shakes her head. "Just scared."

My flashlight reveals a network of booby traps, snares, and trip wires waiting to snag unsuspecting trespassers. It's obvious that whoever put them here was only expecting intruders on foot. I slash them with my sword, then turn to Chapel. "Well, they can't catch my wheels. Hop on. It's safer."

She steps onto the back of my chair and Paul crawls up onto her shoulder, then I roll us down the tunnel as fast as I can while keeping my eyes peeled.

The deeper we go, the more solid the walls become, and they're blanketed in coal dust. The air gets thicker, too, and harder to breathe. My flashlight bounces off something tucked in the wall's hollows. When it doesn't move, I roll toward it.

It's another pile of "treasure"—jewelry and coins, keychains and bottlecaps and broken glass—spilling out of a seam in the wall. "So it *is* demons," I breathe. These tunnels are where they hide out, where they stash what they take. Which means if they took Mama . . .

I scoop up the trinkets and dump them into my backpack with the rest before we roll on. Somewhere up ahead, there's a flickering light that casts spiky shadows on the walls. The torches are closer together, almost as if they're pointing us in the right direction. I feel a surge of hope until I remember something my dad used to say: *Sometimes, the light at the end of the tunnel is an oncoming train.*

In other words, make sure things are getting better before you let your guard down.

The passage veers around a sharp curve and widens again. To the side, I notice smaller tunnels that branch off in different directions. Paul slithers down Chapel's arm, skidding to a stop at the edge of my knee. He raises his fists in a fighting pose.

"What are you gonna do, punch a demon in the ankle?" I tease him.

"So I should just make myself an open target?"

"There's gotta be a middle option."

Paul grumbles but his shoulders loosen.

We roll under what looks like an open doorway and end up in a cavern where limestone formations drip from the ceiling like sharp teeth. The sooty stone walls are bracketed with weathered wooden beams, left over, I'm guessing, from the days when this was a mine shaft. Ropes hang from the ceiling and pool across the ground. And tied to a thick beam in the middle of the room, bound hand to hand to a familiar-looking man, is . . .

"Mama!"

Her eyes are half closed, but when she hears my voice, her head jerks up.

"Jerry! What are you doing here?!"

I roll to her as fast as I can and wrap my arms around her.

"I *knew* something happened," I say. "I knew you wouldn't just leave me."

"Never," she says, her voice cracking as I feel her hot tears drip onto my collar. Then she jerks her face away from mine, her expression hardening. "You have to get out of here! It's not safe!"

My voice is just as hard as hers as I cut her loose, as well as the man next to her. "Not before I rescue you."

She rubs her wrists and winces, holding one of her hands gently in the other. It's twisted and swollen. Then her eyes land on my sword.

"Where did you get that?!" she demands.

"I took it from our house when we moved, and well, when I left to find you I figured I'd need a weapon."

She runs her fingers over Daddy's initials. "It's like our whole family is here," she says.

Then her expression becomes serious. "We have to hurry." She hustles us toward the tunnel. Without bothering to pause, she breathlessly says, "This is Edwin. I helped him escape a trap before we both got caught."

I recognize him as the man from the news.

"You've been fighting these . . . these demons since we arrived in Windy Pines?" I still find it hard to believe.

"I guess you figured it out." She looks behind me and notices Chapel. "And who's this?"

"Chapel Bell. She's . . . my friend."

Chapel smiles. I look over to Paul, who's now perched on her shoulder. I hope I haven't hurt his feelings by leaving him out, but he's smiling, too. He winks and takes a tiny bow before rappelling down the strap of Chapel's overalls and jumping into her bib pocket.

A rustling sound pulls our attention toward the doorway. All the lamps go dark; then the darkness seems to be spilling *in*, shadows breaking off and rushing in to surround us. It's the demons. They were *waiting* for us.

I look around at the little group of people—and one dragon—that I care about more than anything in the world. "Ready?"

They all nod. Chapel squeezes my hand. I take a deep breath and grip my sword, feeling my dad's strength running through the smooth metal. Then I roll forward so I'm face-to-face with the demons and park my chair.

TWENTY-FOUR

ONE DEMON STEPS TOWARD ME AND NARROWS ITS EYES. "WHY have you come here?" it says in a low, screechy voice.

My breath freezes in my throat. The last thing I expected was for them to speak English. Maybe they didn't *want* me to know.

I gulp and nod at Mama. "To rescue my mother."

The demon's eyes flash. "She is no friend of ours." It taps my tire with a claw and grins, flashing a mouthful of sharp teeth. "And neither are you."

Without thinking, I swing my sword, though it's heavier than it looks and hard to control. I don't mean for it to land so close to the demon's fingers but the creature recovers quickly, even though several others rush to its side.

"Stabby-stabby," it calls, wiggling its front claws. "But can a little wheeled one really hurt us with that?"

"I'm no little wheeled one! My name is Jerry." As soon

as it's out of my mouth, I realize telling a demon my name probably wasn't the wisest move.

The demon circles my chair, crawling up and down my wheels and across my push handles. I hold my breath and sit very still, but it doesn't touch me. Instead, it draws a sharp claw down the side of my chair. The sound makes me fold in on myself.

With a satisfied laugh, the demon hops off my chair. "You shouldn't have come here."

"What choice did I have? You took my mother!"

The demon smiles. "And now we have you both."

It nods to the others, who circle Mama, Edwin, and Chapel. Some seize them by their arms and legs while others loop ropes around their bodies. Chapel cries out, "Jerry! Help!"

"Stop!" I shout, drawing my sword. But the demons evade my grasp, climbing the walls, flipping and swinging on the ropes, weaving them around the stalactites and beams into intricate pulleys. The ropes tighten around Mama, Edwin, and Chapel.

I summon my most confident voice and point my sword in the head demon's direction. "Trust me, you don't want to do this."

"Oh, but we *do*!" It cackles.

My eyes drift to my backpack lying open only a foot

away from me. The knots on the broken straps have come undone, and one of the frayed ends flops nearby. I keep my eyes locked on the demon and struggle to reach my pack with one hand, but the threads slip through my fingers. It's enough motion for the bag's contents to rattle, which distracts a few demons. They eye me.

I take a deep breath, steady my arm, and thrust the sword at the backpack. The tip of the blade snags the upper lip, and I flip it toward me. It sails through the air, tossing end over end and scattering jewelry and trinkets everywhere.

The demons dive for the treasures, shoving and scratching one another. That's when I feel something stirring in my pocket. In all the commotion, I hadn't noticed Paul crawl in there, but now he comes rushing out with such force that I think my pocket is going to rip off. He sprints up my arm and takes a leap off my shoulder, flapping his tiny wings toward the ceiling.

Mama and Edwin shriek and look up at Paul with wide eyes. Can they see him?

Paul hovers above, flapping his wings like a humming-bird. Then he dives down and, with a burst of air that seems to travel the entire length of his body, a stream of bluish flame shoots across the ropes, burning through them in seconds.

Mama, Chapel, and Edwin shrug off what's left of the

ropes and run toward me. Paul drifts down and lands in Chapel's outstretched palms. We're off and running, but there's nowhere *to* run.

"Come with me," says a voice from the tunnel entrance. It's a woman's voice, familiar. "Quickly."

A figure steps into the cave and I gasp.

"The Witch of the Woods!" the head demon shrieks at the same time that I blurt, "Miss Mavis?"

TWENTY-FIVE

AS SHE LEADS US INTO ONE OF THE SMALLER CAVES, I NOTICE for the first time how *big* Miss Mavis is. Sitting in my chair, everyone seems tall to me, so sometimes I don't notice people's height. But Miss Mavis is tall enough that she has to fold her body nearly in half to pass through the demon-height doorway. Her shoulders, despite being hunched, are broad and sturdy, her frame packed with muscle. There's a thick leather belt around her waist that's covered in knives and pouches and vials.

"This way," she says. She grabs a torch and presses along the soft stone of the wall, digging her long fingers into the seams until a panel swings inward, revealing a dark passageway. Miss Mavis guides us into the blackness before closing the wall behind her and bracing her back against it.

"We don't have long." She hands the torch to Mama, swings open her coat, and fumbles with the flasks and pouches on her belt. She seems to be pouring together liquids and mixing powders in vials. "I can hold them off for now, but we're outnumbered. They'll get in sooner or later."

There's a loud bang against the other side of the wall and the sound of talons scratching on stone. Miss Mavis's wide eyes dart away from her work, though her hand remains steady. "Probably sooner."

She shifts the containers deftly between her hands, tucking them back into her belt as she finishes each mixture. The row of vials along her waist begins to glow.

"Almost finished." She sprinkles a pinch of herbs into a round glass bottle. The milky liquid within it moves like the ocean. "Leah, I'm going to need your help with this."

"That might be hard," Mama says. She holds out her mangled right hand. "I hurt myself trying to get loose."

"Then, Jerry, you'll help me." It isn't a question. She gathers up two handfuls of the shining vials and shoves them into my arms. While Miss Mavis assembles her ingredients, Edwin tears a strip of flannel off the bottom of his shirt and makes it into a sling for Mama's arm and hand.

"This work has been in my family for more than a hundred years," Miss Mavis says. "Five generations, but I'm the last of my bloodline. I've been training your mother ever since y'all got here and now I'll train you. Not exactly ideal circumstances, but we work with what we got."

"So *you're* the witch." When I heard the radio voices talking about a witch, the last thing I would have pictured was Miss Mavis. "The one they talk about on the late-night radio."

Miss Mavis straightens her spine proudly, unfolding to her impressive height, towering over us like a sequoia. "My great-great-great-grandmother was the original Witch of the Woods back when Windy Pines was founded. She hid there when the townspeople ran her out because they were scared of her magic. She passed her work down to her daughter, and then she passed it to hers . . . and so on, down to me. It was my mother, actually, who started the motel as a cover. She ran it in the daytime and did our family's work by night." Miss Mavis looks off into the distance, even though it's too dark in here to see three feet in front of us. In the torchlight, the lines of her face smooth until she looks oddly young. And . . . afraid?

She shakes her head. "But I'm too old to fight, and I don't have a daughter. So I found someone to take over our work: your mother." She finally looks down at me. "I was looking specifically for a woman who had a daughter. And my instincts told me you two would be the right fit."

"Wait. Does that mean *I'm* supposed to be next?"

She smiles. "If you want to be."

"But . . ." How did she think I was going to be a demon fighter when most people don't think I can do anything?

"You've already proven me right," she says. "How brave you are. How well you can problem solve. I guess it makes sense. You've already had to do a lot of that, haven't you?"

She's not wrong. I've gotten good at it because I *had* to.

"So your family's work," I say tentatively, "is killing demons?"

Miss Mavis huffs and straightens her spine. "Who said anything about killing?" she says. "We never *killed* anyone. And those creatures"—she gestures at the wall, the claws still scrabbling on the other side of it —"aren't *demons*, exactly. They're, well . . . I'll try to explain quickly." She bites her lip. Shoving the remaining bottles back into their holsters, she motions for Mama to hand her the torch. She crouches on the dirt floor and scratches a stick figure in the dust with the unlit end of the pole.

"Now, see, when people die, and they have . . . unfinished business, so to speak, and they're not ready to let go of the living world, their spirits leave their bodies"—she draws what looks like a little Halloween ghost—"but they still hang around for a while. Sometimes, those spirits find peace, and they move on. But if they don't . . ." Her bushy gray brows knit together.

Chapel's eyes shine in the torchlight. "So the shadow monsters are *real* ghosts?" she says barely above a whisper.

"Well, yes, you could say so. At least, they start out that way. But then some of them want to hold on too long."

Miss Mavis scratches out the ghost in the dirt. "And the more they try, the more they lose themselves. Turn into . . . something else." With the back of her hand, she brushes away the dust from the scratched-out ghost. "To keep holding on, they have to draw life energy from something. At first it's objects people have touched that they've transferred some of their energy to."

Now it makes sense why they collected trash and junk along with things that were valuable. All that really mattered was the human energy attached to them.

"But after time, that's not enough. The earth wants to let go of them. They don't want to let go of it. So what do they do?" She pulls back the torch so we can see her new drawing. Now there are waves radiating off the stick figure and into the outstretched hands of a spiny, shadowy creature. "They pull the life force directly from people, until those people become spirits themselves. But because so much has been taken from the dead, they can't leave this earth, either. So, they become what *they* are." She taps the demon drawing. "Spirits who've become twisted and corrupt. Now all they know how to do is *take*."

That feeling when the demons touched me, that fuzzy sensation—they must have taken my energy. Maybe they were going to keep draining me until there was nothing left. I shiver. "I think they took some of mine."

"So let me get this straight," Chapel says. "Those things

out there, you're saying they're *ghost-mons*?"

Miss Mavis sighs. "So now you know why I'm not here to kill them," she says. "They're already dead, in a sense. My family's work has been freeing them. We find the spirit underneath all that hate and anger and greed, and we release them from their hold on this world."

"And what happens after that?" Chapel asks.

Miss Mavis hands her the torch and stands up. With a shrug, she grabs the biggest vial on her belt and raises it into the air. "That's not up to us."

Motioning all of us behind her, Miss Mavis leans into the wall. She signals for me to hand back the bottles and stashes them in her belt. Outside, the scratching has died down. It's almost *too* quiet. Miss Mavis kicks open the door, and a row of demons scatters back as we move into the massive cavern.

The sparkly items from my backpack are strewn across the floor, and the rest of the demons hover possessively over what they've claimed.

Chapel tugs on my sleeve. "Why do they still want that, if they've already sucked the energy out of it?"

"I don't know," I whisper.

Miss Mavis hands each of us a stone. Mine is no bigger than my palm and a deep, mossy green, smooth but not polished.

She slips her stone into her belt and raises her hand,

shouting something that sounds like, "Univertus!"

A bolt of white-hot energy shoots from her hand, blurring into blue at the edges. The ground shakes and the walls start to crumble as the edges of the bedrock *lift up*. A few demons scurry away, escaping out the tunnel the way we came, but most slip to the center of the cavern.

I lock my brakes and Chapel holds on to me while Miss Mavis leans into the curve of the floor. On the other side of me, Mama and Edwin do the same. They slide their stones into their pockets. Chapel puts hers in the side of her shoe like a lucky penny. I drop mine into my jacket pocket, feel it nestle against my dad's bandanna patch next to my heart.

Miss Mavis calls out, "Now!" and the corners of the room drop back down. She grabs Mama's hand and steps forward. As Edwin moves in closer, gently hooking his fingers around Mama's in her sling, I understand what we have to do.

I take Chapel's hand on one side and Miss Mavis's on the other, and we all move in and close the circle. The stone in my pocket warms as our hands connect. Through my jacket pocket, it's glowing.

"Whatever you do—whatever *they* do—don't let go!" Miss Mavis shouts. "They can't hurt you as long as the circle remains unbroken! The stone—from the bedrock of this land—it contains them!"

The demons are now piled on top of one another. Chapel squeezes my hand, two tight squeezes, like a promise.

Miss Mavis starts chanting in a language I don't know. Her words sound like a mix of the Latin in my encyclopedias and the Hebrew I would mumble at my grandparents' temple.

"Levitorum!" The vials from her belt begin to glow, emitting beams of light that connect to the stones in our pockets. The vessels rise up and float in the air, then quickly crash to the ground, releasing streaks of mist and smoke. I wince but keep a firm grip on the hands holding mine.

My hair blows back from my face. Miss Mavis keeps chanting, but it's hard to hear her voice over the roar of the wind. A sudden gust rushes between me and Chapel, and I lose my grip on her hand.

The rock in my pocket goes cold. I reach for Chapel but my hands grab empty air; the wind is just too strong. A demon leaps from the pile, aiming for the break in the circle.

Then I feel something slithering on my arm. I squeeze my eyes shut, waiting for the fuzzy sensation, the draining to begin. One of them has me.

I grasp desperately for Chapel's hand, pulling myself through the wind like I'm trying to swim against a current. Whatever's touching my arm wraps its talons around me. A pulse of warmth spreads across my chest. I open my eyes.

Between Chapel and me—tail coiled around my wrist, both hands gripping Chapel's thumb with every bit of strength in his tiny body—is Paul.

"Revinitim!" Miss Mavis shouts.

The demons freeze. Slowly, transparent human shapes rise from their bodies. The outline of a man with a ginger beard and a hard hat separates from one; as it does, a gold watch floats up from the pile on the floor and settles onto his wrist. Across from him, a boy and girl—about twenty years old—emerge from their gargoyle forms holding video cameras. One of the smallest demon bodies releases a wisp of a little kid in a scout uniform.

The demon who lunged for me, the same one who spoke to me earlier, is frozen in midair, face contorted. From behind its body drifts the silhouette of a girl who looks close to my age, though she's almost the same height as me sitting in my chair. She has long black hair and an old-fashioned blue dress. A familiar pendant rises from the floor and settles around her neck.

Millie Dobbs.

Her face, pale and solemn, hovers inches from mine.

"You're one of them," I whisper. "They got you, too."

She screws up her face. "Nobody *got* me. I was here first."

My jaw falls. "You?"

"Daddy told me not to play in the mines." Millie's eyes flash.

"But why did you do it?" I ask. "Why did you take the others?"

"I was alone for so long. I was so cold. So I found a way to . . ." She looks around at the other ghosts. "Not be alone anymore."

The jewelry and keys and even the trash still float around us. Twisting my arm so I'm still touching Chapel's with my elbow, I pluck my sword out of the air and rub the dust from Daddy's initials. As the wind dies down, static crackles over the radio. I press the headphones to my ear and adjust the dial.

WE HAVE BEEN LEFT NO CHOICE, says a rumbling voice. *WE MUST MOVE.*

Then the static blurs until the words are so distorted, I can barely understand, no matter how I turn the dial. Move *what?*

There's a great ripping sound, like the earth is being torn in half. The cavern shakes violently.

Rocks tumble from the walls; stalactites crack loose from the ceiling and spear the ground like toothpicks. During earthquake drills at school, the kids who walked were taught to huddle on the floor, but teachers just had me park my chair against a wall and cover my head. I look around for a wall that doesn't seem to be in danger of caving in, but there isn't one.

A voice growls through the gap, carried on a wind so strong it kicks dust into my eyes. *IT IS TIME.*

The voice is familiar. It's one I've heard on the radio.

"Time for *what?*" Chapel yells, but the roar overhead swallows her voice and whatever is above us either doesn't hear or chooses not to answer.

The walls shake and the support beams splinter and fall, crashing into the torches and lanterns. They unleash flames that gobble up the wood and spread along the walls, hungry for more.

The ghosts fly around our heads. Their human bodies, transparent, swoop and dive like seagulls.

"No!" I scream.

But it's too late. They are sucked back into the demon bodies, which spring to life, milling around in a frenzy under the falling debris.

The room around us is a smashed shambles, the broken torches tipping into one another and exploding into fireballs. I roll as fast as I can toward the tunnel's mouth, Chapel grabbing my handles to race out with me. Paul clings to my shoulder and Mama reaches out to pull Edwin through the chaos of crashing wood planks and stones. The demons scramble out after us, leapfrogging over one another.

We sprint down the tunnel just as what's left of the cave crumbles, taking trees from above down with it. The deeper we get, the *fresher* this part of the tunnel seems, as if someone's just finished digging it. The glow from my flashlight barely helps; the all-swallowing dark of the tunnel narrows it to a sliver. The only good thing is that we seem to have lost the demons somewhere—they're no longer behind us.

I touch the worm-wet walls until my hand hits a ridge of sharp metal that feels like the edge of a tin can. It slices my palm. The metal rim leads to an open hole in the wall. I reach my hand in and feel more ridged metal. A culvert.

"This way." I roll into the tube, my wheels echoing down the corrugated metal walls. It's just barely wide enough for my chair; the others have to crawl through. Even I have to duck my head.

It seems like we're moving forever, though it's probably not more than twenty minutes. We're all quiet, which just makes it feel even longer.

"What *was* that?" I finally ask to fill the silence.

"I'll tell you everything, I promise. As soon as we get to safety." Mama's voice sounds strangely calm.

Just when it starts to feel like the culvert will never end, I see a light. Or rather, a splotch of darkness that's not quite as dark as the surrounding tunnels. When we get closer, I notice it's coming from above. The culvert slants sharply upward, nearly vertical at the end where the opening is. Now that we're directly under it, I realize the light has been coming through slats in a round grate cover. "A storm drain," I murmur under my breath.

I glance at Chapel, who seems to be thinking the same thing as me. "I'll climb out first," she says.

"No way." Mama shakes her head. "I'll go."

"With your arm?" Edwin steps forward. "I'm going."

"It can't be either of y'all." Chapel points up at the grate. "To get that cover off from the inside, we need someone whose hands are small enough to fit through the holes." She flexes her fingers triumphantly, flashing the Band-Aids wrapped around three of her fingers. She braces her arms against the side of the culvert, locks one sneaker into the ridged metal, and freezes.

I look up. A shadow moves, crawling across the moonlight and coming to rest again. It's an orb weaver, a huge spider suspended in a zigzag-patterned web. Chapel's foot falters, slipping off the metal.

"Wait," I say. "Chapel can't go first. She has to help y'all lift my chair out." I smile at her. She exhales. "It has to be me."

Mama's eyes dart between my face and my wheels, concern wrinkling her brow. I take her hand, the one with the two rings, and squeeze it. "Trust me."

She bites her lip and nods. "Okay."

I shimmy out of my chair. Grabbing the ridges of the wall, I pull myself up to standing. I lean against the metal, cool on my skin, and then grab the next groove up. It's hard without full use of my legs and arms. But every time I slip, I feel hands below bracing me. I look down and see Chapel's grinning face.

Finally I hit metal. The grate is thick, solid, not like the soup-can sides of the culvert. It's rough under my fingers, and the scrape of my nails against it sends a bone-chattering shudder through me. A week ago—even a few days ago—I wouldn't have dreamed of trying to move it. But now, I believe I can.

Threading my fingers through the holes and wrapping them around the bars, I push up with every bit of strength I've got. It takes about a minute, and I have to rest, but finally it pops loose. After shoving the cover aside and hooking my arms over the lip of the pipe, I grab the ground and heave my body out.

I find a twig and carefully scoop up the orb weaver in her web, then crawl to a tangle of brush and set her down.

When I get back to the edge of the pipe, I see Chapel below me, unspooling one of the demons' ropes out of a pocket of my backpack. I clench my fist in a silent cheer. Of *course* she would think to grab that! She tosses me one end of the rope. I catch it and hold on as tight as I can.

Chapel threads the rope around my chair, making a kind of pulley, then ties the other loose end of the rope around her waist.

Edwin lifts her onto his shoulders and she loops her elbows through mine as Edwin gives her a big push, enough for me to pull her the rest of the way over the lip. Once we're both steady on the ground, Chapel and I pull back on the ropes. They prick and burn against my palms, but through the opening I see my chair rising toward us. When I hear the frame scrape against the lip of the drain, I pull as hard as I can. It finally comes flying up onto the dirt beside us.

Edwin boosts Mama out next, who is favoring her broken hand while still protesting that she could have done it herself, and he crawls out after her. Then there's a crash from down in the tunnel, like a small avalanche, and a moment later Miss Mavis surfaces, seemingly unscathed. Mama kicks the drain cover back into place. I know it's too late, like locking the door of a burning house, but I get why she does it.

We've popped out into pine needles and red dirt near the tree line. I scoot up into my chair and squint through the gaps in the trees. The glow from the fire is bright enough for us to see the caved-in ground, the flames licking up red and angry from the hole where the mine used to be. I wonder if the rest of the tunnels could catch fire and sink down with it. I wonder where the demons are, if they crawled up another tunnel.

"Uh, Jerry?" Paul mutters in my ear. "Is that mountain . . . *moving?*"

TWENTY-SIX

I LOOK IN THE DIRECTION HE'S POINTING. THERE IS INDEED A mountain in the trees, and it's *rising*. Worse than that is the ground shuddering underneath us like an earthquake. The thing—the mountain—is actually walking toward us. Then its cliffs separate clearly into five stone bodies, human shaped and stocky, with massive limbs. They reach down with arms that ripple with thick muscles, snapping tree trunks, kicking at trails, and strewing dust everywhere.

One rips up a tree root as if it's pulling a thread from a sweater. It splits the ground in front of me, snagging my wheel on a branch. Suddenly I'm whipped through the air, Chapel still clinging to my handles, and we hit the hard-packed dirt with a teeth-rattling *thud*.

My body feels whiplashed but I shake it off. "Are you okay?" I ask Chapel.

"Um, not really," she mutters. "What *are* those things?"

There's no time to answer because debris is flying toward us from all angles; I duck as a huge boulder narrowly misses my chair. I grab my rims and try to steer away but end up doing a tight turn instead. Dust from the ground sprays around us in a wide arc, then floats in the air.

"Look!" Chapel shouts. The creatures standing closest to us stumble, streams of water rolling down their rocky faces. Is it the dust?

It gives me an idea.

"Hang on tight!" I lean forward and spin my wheels again while the dust kicks up around us. Then I cut figure eights on the forest floor, stirring up as much dust as possible, until we can no longer see the sky. When we come to a stop, I draw my sword and stab it into a patch of soft moss on what looks like a stone foot.

The creature flinches with a howl that echoes through the clouds. I have just enough time to yank my sword back before it pulls up its foot, which lands with ground-shaking force a few feet away. I manage to dodge it and roll sideways, then wedge my blade into a patch of silty soil.

The sounds around us are chaotic, the scrape of stone falling into stone and the great roar of wind. Then comes a thunderous crash that sounds like an avalanche. Rocks roll across the ground, small at first, then bigger and bigger.

As a grapefruit-sized rock rolls to a stop against one of my front casters, I realize that I've just watched one of the things fall.

"What *was* that?" Chapel murmurs in my ear.

I stare at the sword in my hands. Did *I* take down a mountain monster?

The very same rocks roll in circles, stacking themselves on top of one another until the creature stands at full height again. Crags of rock hanging from its side curl into a massive fist.

Whatever these things are, I'm not sure they're here to fight us. I don't think they can even see us through the dust, and they're so huge that we must feel like ants biting them. Even when they topple, they promptly reassemble themselves, rising above the woods in massive black mounds.

Then the ground moves, and Chapel, Paul, and I are lifted above the trees. Bewildered, I look around with panic as we rise higher and higher. The moss and ferns we'd been standing on fall away, leaving us on hard stone. It forms a kind of platform, like an elevator with no walls. The edges of the stone curl up, cupping us in a kind of basin. Shallow fissures run across the surface and crevices separate sections of the wall into pillars, almost like . . . *fingers*. We are sitting inside a giant hand.

Soon we're close enough to look whatever it is in the face. A crystalline eye blinks. It's as tall as one of the walls in our motel room and twice as far across.

Finally, the hand stops moving. The mountain reverberates with a deep growl that sounds like rocks rolling against one another.

The voice from the radio. *IT IS TIME.*

TWENTY-SEVEN

"I KNOW WHAT YOU ARE." IT'S OBVIOUS NOW THAT I'D HEARD ITS voice. My hands grip the rims of my wheels until my knuckles go numb, but I keep my voice steady. "You're a Guardian."

THAT I AM, the hill monster rumbles. *I AM GEVIG'DOR. YOU MAY CALL ME GEVI.*

I pull myself to the tallest height I can manage in my chair and pick up my sword. "Don't hurt us!"

WE HURT NO ONE. GUARDIANS ARE PROTEC-TORS.

"Protectors of what?" I ask.

OF THE FOREST, says another voice. A long row of them stands shoulder to shoulder: a dark mountain range blocking the moonlight.

THIS WOOD IS FILLED WITH THINGS OLDER THAN YOU CAN IMAGINE, Gevi continues. *BUT WE*

*ARE OLDER YET. WE SAW ITS TALLEST TREE
GROW FROM A SAPLING. WE WATCH OVER IT.
FOR MANY YEARS THERE WAS PEACE. BALANCE.
THEN THEY CAME.*

"Who came?" asks Chapel.

THE BEASTS.

"They weren't always here?"

*FOR MANY YEARS, IT WAS ONLY US, AND THE
TREES, AND THE ANIMALS. AND WILD THINGS
WE SHELTERED HERE. THEN, THE WITCH.*

"Miss Mavis!"

*SHE IS THE LAST OF HER LINE. THE FIRST
CAME LONG AGO. SHE BECAME A PART OF THIS
WOOD. SHE HELPED US PROTECT IT. IN RETURN,
WE GRANTED HER HAVEN FROM THOSE WHO
MEANT HER HARM.*

"Symbiosis," Chapel says. Paul and I look at her. That's
not a word I've learned yet. "It was good for the witch *and*
the Guardians for her to be here," she explains.

"Yeah, well, you left the last of the magic bloodline
down there in the dirt," Paul mutters, craning his neck in
search of Miss Mavis.

"Paul!" I close my hand around his mouth.

YOUR FRIEND IS RIGHT, Gevi booms. *BUT I
ASSURE YOU, SHE IS SAFE, ALONG WITH LEAH.*

Hearing Mama's name gives me the strength to roll closer.

"She's my mother," I say quietly. I'm not even sure Gevi's heard me until I feel his palm vibrate under my wheels. "Leah," I say, louder. "The helper."

WE OWE HER A GREAT DEBT, Gevi says.

"Wait." Chapel squints up at him. "If you're here to protect the forest, why are you tearing it up?"

Gevi sighs, a sound like wind blowing through a canyon. *THERE HAS BEEN A BREACH,* he says finally. *THE BEASTS HAVE FOUND THEIR WAY OUT. THE BARRIERS HOLDING THEM IN THIS WOOD HAVE WORN THIN.*

Gevi pauses. *THEY WILL DRAIN THE LIFE FROM ALL LIVING THINGS.*

"So why don't you stop them?"

Gevi smiles. *WE CANNOT. THEY ARE BEYOND THE FOREST LINE. WE ARE HERE TO WARN YOU. IT IS YOU WHO MUST STOP THEM.*

"Me?" I ask. "But how?"

Another smile, then Gevi starts walking, a movement that feels surprisingly smooth from our perch in his hand. As he takes step after massive step, the treetops brush the giant's craggy shoulders. Before long, we're back at the edge of the woods. Spread out below us, glowing in the middle of an island of asphalt, is the Slumbering Giant Motel.

OUR JOB IS DONE. IT IS IN YOUR HANDS.

"But, what—"

Before I can finish, Gevi gently deposits us on the ground. Then he steps back behind the tree line, branches closing behind him like curtains, and stands shoulder to shoulder with the other Guardians, sentry still.

TWENTY-EIGHT

I ROLL TO MAMA AND THROW MY ARMS AROUND HER. "ARE YOU okay?"

"We're fine, baby. But look—"

Even though the sky is starting to lighten, the motel parking lot is filled with shadows. Shadows that are moving, closing in around the building. Next to me, Chapel stiffens.

The demons are streaming out of the ground—the drainpipe we crawled out from, or another like it—directly outside the forest. Now they're everywhere: climbing walls, scratching at doors and windows, and perching on the roof looking for a way in through the air vents.

"Daddy! Mama!" Chapel starts to run up the slope toward the lot.

Miss Mavis catches the tail of Chapel's jacket. "Wait! I know you're scared. But we *can't* go charging in there without a plan."

"She's right," Mama agrees. "First we have to get everyone out safely—"

Something pops into my head. "I think I know how to do that."

"Then we need to trap the demons in one place so we can release them," finishes Miss Mavis.

"That might not be too hard." Chapel points toward the edge of the trees where more demons are flooding from the storm drain and rushing toward the motel. "They're all heading to the same place."

"They're out." Miss Mavis nods gravely. "I caved in the tunnel behind us to block them in, but I knew it would only slow them down. Once they'd broken through . . ." She shakes her head. "The time to stop them from leaving the forest has passed."

"So what can we do?" Chapel cries out. "There are people up there! My *family* is up there! They're going to drain them, all of them!"

"Do you trust me?" I ask.

"Of course!"

"No," I say, meeting my mother's eyes. "I meant you, Mama. Do *you* trust me?"

Mama takes a deep breath and nods. "Yes, Jerry. I trust you."

"Then push me up this hill."

Mama gives me a sharp look. I sigh. She *is* still my

mother. "Please?"

With her good hand on one of my handles while I push from my rims at the same time, Mama boosts me over the steep slope and onto the pavement. The others run alongside me as I dodge behind the parked cars, trying to stay out of the demons' sight.

We make it to the niche behind the office, the gate leading to Miss Mavis's apartment. It feels like a lifetime ago that I rolled through that gate looking for Mama. But something I noticed then is still there: a small red metal box covered in glass.

I look around for a rock or a thick piece of wood before I remember Miss Mavis's stone. I pull it out of my pocket and smash it against the box, shattering the glass, and yank down the small white lever inside. The scream of a fire alarm fills the parking lot.

Doors open around the motel. People lean out of their windows to see what the commotion is about. I start to shout a warning, but then I realize the demons are cringing and cowering, covering their ears.

"They hate the sound," I whisper. At least it will slow them down, but people aren't heeding the alarm's warnings. A few even shrug and step back inside, closing their doors once they see there's no fire.

"It's a real fire they want, is it?" Paul huffs, jumping from my pocket and crawling up onto my shoulder. He tries to blow another stream of flame, but only a rusty rattle of air comes out.

I grab him by the tail before he can try again. "Paul, no!"

As I'm stuffing him back into my pocket, I feel everyone's eyes on me.

"Y'all can see him?"

Chapel nods. Mama, Edwin, and Miss Mavis do, too.

"I thought he was only visible in the woods?"

"The forest's energy is powerful," Miss Mavis says. "It made him stronger." She extends a hand to him. "Come here. I need your help."

Paul eyes her warily but obliges. She holds him up to a smoke detector I hadn't noticed, tucked in a corner of the awning above us.

"Okay, think *really* hot, and then scorch it!" she says.

I start to ask what difference it'll make when I've already set off the fire alarm, but then Paul takes a deep breath and blows out the second-biggest flame of his life. Immediately, there's a blood-curdling shriek from inside the motel.

Ten seconds later, doors slam open again, and this time, the occupants scramble out soaking wet. The ceiling sprinklers inside the rooms have drenched them.

"Everyone, hurry!" I shout. "Get away from here. As fast as you can!"

Some people start to argue, but their expressions change

once they notice the demons. Mr. Bell comes racing out of his room, followed by a woman I assume is Chapel's mom.

Chapel runs toward them. "Daddy! Mama!"

"Baby!" Chapel's mom cries. "You're safe! You're okay!"

She and Mr. Bell start to dart down the stairs, but a group of demons emerges from below and blocks their path.

Chapel freezes.

"Stay back, baby!" Mrs. Bell screams. The demons advance toward them, claws extended. Shrinking back, the Bells climb back up the stairs and run into their room, slamming the door.

Chapel starts after them, and I roll to her side. "Don't!"

"But my parents—"

"I know. But if you chase them, they'll get you. We'll figure this out another way. Come on!"

Nearby, Miss Mavis casts some sort of spell, and a line of purplish light beams out in front of her, one that pushes against the demons like a plow. She's able to corral them back, through an open door and into an empty room.

But this is just one group. There are so many, and they seem to multiply the more Miss Mavis and Mama and Edwin try to contain them. There are demons swinging from the roof gutters, shattering windows, and bending wrought-iron railings.

"This won't hold them for long!" Mama shouts as she

slams another door. "They keep escaping. We have to release them now!"

"We need a circle of stones," says Miss Mavis. "Jerry!"

But all I see in the parking lot are scattered pebbles and bits of broken glass. I wish I hadn't lost my rock collection back in the woods. Then something occurs to me.

"What if a Guardian could be our circle?" I ask.

Miss Mavis shakes her head. "They don't leave the forest line. They never have."

"The *mountains* don't leave the forest," I say. "But mountains are *made* of stones, of boulders. And back in the forest, they kept falling down and getting back up. Could Gevi—I don't know—disassemble himself somehow?"

Miss Mavis shakes her head again. "Too risky. For as long as anyone's been around to know about it, these woods have operated on a kind of code. You're asking to break its laws. That'll come at a cost."

"But Mavis, what we're doing here"—Mama gestures to the demons swooping into rooms— "it's not enough."

"Please. We have to try," Chapel adds, tearfully. "My parents are trapped."

Miss Mavis squeezes her eyes shut, then nods. "Fine. But Jerry, this is your idea. Ask them yourself." Her brow creases behind her glasses. "And be warned, you might not like the answer."

I don't even think about it. In a flash, I'm rolling down

179

the hill and back at the tree line. The others run after me.

Once I'm there, I park my chair. "Gevi! I need you! I know you can't cross the tree line. But you and the other Guardians *can* help! We need stones to contain them. You—you have stones." I point up at him desperately. "If you surround the motel, my mother and Miss Mavis can free the demons."

The silence that follows is so loud it roars in my ears.

"Please, Gevi! I know you want to help. This is how you can. Please!"

No response. Then something else occurs to me. I try one last thing.

"The woods contain old and dark things." I echo Gevi. "I know that's what you do. You keep them in the woods, where the world is safe from them." I look into the brilliant orb of the morning sun just peeking above the trees, imagining it's Gevi's all-seeing eye. "You keep *them* safe. From us. And everything out here." I jerk my head in the direction of the swarming motel. "If we don't stop these things, *nothing* will be safe. Not outside the woods *or* in."

Silence. I stare up at the mountains, glowing in the sunrise. I think I can even make out Gevi's face.

Then, a great rumbling. The ground trembles. And a boulder taller than me rolls out of the forest. It's followed by another, and another. I stare at the mountains.

In a move so quick, so deft and subtle that I almost miss

it, Gevi shrugs a shoulder and a ripple of stones moves. They rumble loose and roll down his arm, down the forest path, toward us.

Behind me, Chapel whoops. Miss Mavis smiles.

Stone by stone, Gevi crumbles until there's nothing left. The stones that were once him form a complete circle, surrounding the motel. The last one rolls in a figure eight until it comes to a rest next to my chair. I press my hand to it, feeling its energy. "Thank you."

Miss Mavis looks at me with an unreadable expression and nods. We follow her until we are right outside the circle of stones. She takes charms from her belt, opening the vials and spilling them on the asphalt. Miss Mavis lays her hand on a boulder the size of a small car, leans her head down until her forehead nearly touches it, takes a deep breath, and begins the incantation again.

As wind kicks up inside the circle, Miss Mavis's steel-gray hair springs free from its pins and lifts off her shoulders, wiry and wild. On the other side, the trees thrash and break. Miss Mavis strains her voice to chant louder against the noise. Cradling her smashed hand against her chest, Mama joins in, her own voice clear and strong.

Once again, spirits rise from the demons' bodies and float above the treetops like smoke. I notice the faint outline of a logger, a man like Edwin, like my dad. His shadow grows misty and fades into the sky as he drifts up and joins a line of fog. It comprises the spirits of loggers and campers, lost travelers and teenagers who went in search of urban legends.

Hundreds of shadow bodies rise, their silhouettes swirling into one another, and then the giant mass lifts to the sky and they're gone. Their demon forms, frozen in poses of attack, crumble into piles of ash. The motel windows blacken with soot and I know the demons inside have met the same fate.

Only one spirit is left hovering near the ground. Long black hair and clenched fists, eyes squeezed shut. Miss Mavis repeats the last line of her spell.

But Millie's spirit stays put.

TWENTY-NINE

MAMA PLEADS, "LET GO."

Millie shakes her head. "I can't."

Chapel ducks between Mama and Mavis and stands in front of Millie, her face solemn and determined.

"You're scared," she says. "I know you don't want to be alone. But the others are gone."

"Where did they go?" Millie jerks her chin upward. "What comes after this?"

"I don't know," Chapel admits. "I wish I did. But none of us do."

"I wasn't ready to leave." Millie's fists clench tighter.

"I understand that," Chapel says softly. "But you don't want to stay here. Not like this. And—"

"And I don't want to be *that*." Millie looks down. We follow her eyes to the frozen form of her demon body, just inside Gevi's circle. The body cracks. Rather than dissolve into dust, it falls apart in reluctant, heavy chunks, like something is still trying to hold it together.

She's about to let go, I think.

Then a monstrous roar knocks the wind out of me. Something slams into me from behind, and a strange feeling wraps around my ribs, as if my bones are trying to flee my skin.

I try to open my mouth to scream but my mouth won't open.

Suddenly I'm lifted out of my seat and into the air. I reach back and grab for my chair, but my arms are frozen; whatever has me is too strong. My arms and legs begin to move like I'm swimming, but I'm not moving them. Worst of all, I'm charging at Chapel, trying to grab at her with outstretched hands.

"Jerry!" Chapel shrieks. "What are you doing?"

"Jerry's not here." The voice that comes out of my mouth isn't mine. "You're with *me* now."

It sounds nothing like the scared little girl from a moment ago, but I know it's Millie, and that she's somehow inside me. *Stop!* I think, hoping she can hear me. *Let me go!* Her essence twines around my skeleton like a vine. Inside me, she's not a kid anymore; she's a dark force of shadows and spite. I wonder if she can drain me from the inside, take everything that's *me* until all that's left is my body.

I concentrate on pulling back, trying to stop her from

moving my arms and legs. Yet my fingers wrap around Chapel's arms, my nails dig into her skin.

But Chapel stands firm. She removes my nails from her flesh, cups my face in her own hands, and looks deep into my eyes, like she's trying to look *past* them somehow.

"Jerry. I know you're in there."

I am, I think. But I can't make my mouth say the words.

"You have to make her leave. Kick her out."

Get out, I think. *Let go of me! Get out!*

Instead, Millie's shadow digs in deeper. "I don't think so," she says. It's my own jaw moving as she speaks. "You're mine now. And we will always be together. We won't ever be alone again."

Chapel steps back a few paces, then slips her hand into her pocket. There's a bright flash; then I see what's tucked in her palm: the stone that Miss Mavis gave her.

Struggling against the force holding me back, I move toward Chapel like I'm swimming through jelly. My limbs are now frozen, clutched to my sides like I'm wrapped in a straitjacket, but slowly, slowly I'm able move them. It feels like forever, but finally I'm able to reach out my hand to clutch hers.

A shock jolts up my arm as I press my palm to the polished stone. Inside me, Millie screams. Even without a circle, the stone has enough power to loosen her hold on me.

Chapel's eyes meet mine, and she nods toward my own pocket. Grabbing my stone seems impossible, but I have to try, especially now that Millie has been weakened. My arm feels like its dragging through sand, but eventually I'm able to pull it out of my pocket. With her free hand, Chapel grabs mine and presses her warm palm to the cool stone. Static crackles like lighting through my veins. The two of us are a circle now.

Millie's wails rip through my ears from the inside out. She pushes against my skin so hard; I fear she might break through at any moment.

"Jerry," Chapel says. I look into the calm, dark brown velvet of her eyes. "This isn't gonna be enough. You must make her leave."

"I can't." The pressure of her under my skin is so strong it hurts. I'm afraid she's going to tear me to pieces.

"Yes, you can. You can do a lot of things. That's why I like you." She grins, her dimples digging into her cheeks. "You can *almost* keep up with me!"

I manage a shaky smile before I close my eyes and clamp my hands down hard on Chapel's.

"Get out," I say, barely above a whisper.

I feel Millie waver. She's a shimmer on a hot blacktop, a vapor around a can of gasoline.

Squeezing even harder, I take a deep breath and say, with every drop of conviction I've got, "Get. *Out.*"

My breath is pulled right out of me, along with what feels like half my guts. I hit the ground so fast I don't even realize I'm falling until I'm on the concrete.

Instead of towering tower over us, Millie's ghost form is small and pale, curled up on the ground. She's crying, *sobbing*, and her sobs really do sound like the wind in the trees. "I want to go home. I want to go," she cries.

But where would *home* be? Some house that's long ago been torn down? Her family? Would any of them even still be alive?

Chapel's eyes remain steady as she steps toward the weeping form. She reaches out a hand and Millie takes it. Even though Chapel's hand passes right through hers, Millie smiles like she can feel it. I hold out my own hand. Millie's palm is a cold breeze.

Her spirit form flickers and fades. The cracked pieces of her demon body sift into black sand. With a blinding flash of light, her spirit streaks into the sky. A great wind blows, causing Millie's demon ashes to dance in the air.

I scoop up a handful of the ash. It filters through my fingers, silky and fine.

"It didn't hurt her," Miss Mavis says. "That wasn't *her*. It was just a shell. She's already gone."

We stand together in a line, just outside the circle of stones, and watch her streak of light fade into the trees.

THIRTY

WE REMAIN LIKE THAT FOR A FEW MINUTES, JUST WATCHING THE sky. Finally, Miss Mavis turns to me.

"I really did mean to hire a housekeeper," she says. "I placed a want ad. But when your mother answered, just talking to her over the phone, I could . . . *sense* you, the power you hold. You show it already. Your gift of conjuring—"

I look over at Paul perched on my shoulder. "I *told* them he was real!"

"I *told* you I was real!" Paul shouts at the same time.

Miss Mavis steps forward and rests her hand on the stones that were once Gevi. "Thank you," she says. "My protector. My friend."

"Miss Mavis?" I say softly, wheeling up to her. "What really happened?"

She sighs. "I left a few things out of my story before. I grew up in these woods, in the shadow of the Guardians."

A smile. "My mother did the work of the Witch of the Woods, and I was her apprentice. I wasn't much older than you then. And I was getting good at it, too . . . until I lost her. Same as you lost your mama. Except I never found mine."

"Then why didn't you tell me the truth when I came looking for her?"

"She made me promise not to. She wanted to keep you safe."

My head swirls with more questions, ones I can't find the words for. "What happened to you? When they couldn't find your mama?"

"For a while I tried to do her work on my own. But I wasn't ready. Mostly, I hid out in our house in the woods. It was protected by spells, so nothing could find me that I didn't want to."

I recall the little house in the woods, how the demons couldn't cross the moss yard.

She continues, "I was found eventually and taken from the woods. I had no other relatives, so I ended up bouncing around local church families and the county home. I came back to claim the motel when I was twenty-one. It was rightfully mine, left to me by my mama, and it was an empty wreck then, but I got it up and running."

"Did you come back to be the Witch of the Woods?"

She shakes her head. "I know it was wrong, but I couldn't

bear to return to the woods. I . . . I left them unprotected." Her shoulders droop. "The beasts started taking people again."

"So you hired Mama."

Miss Mavis nods, leaning against the boulder. "I never forgot you," she says softly.

The rocks begin to glow, almost pulsing with energy. Then they roll over the edge of the asphalt and back to the tree line where they tumble toward each other, stacking to form Gevi once again. He towers above us, still and silent, watching.

"What happens now?" I ask.

She adjusts her belt and looks at me. "My grandmother's house is still here. I was thinking of moving back in. Retiring from retiring, I guess you could say. When—*if*—you decide, you are always welcome to visit and learn more." She tilts her head to the side. "Not because you're Leah's daughter. Because you're you."

I smile. "Okay."

Miss Mavis tips her chin in Chapel's direction. "Your friend, too, if she wants. She has quite the talent for communicating with spirits."

"What about the motel?" Mama asks, wrapping her arms around my shoulders.

Miss Mavis laughs. "You can run it if you want. You'd do a better job than I did. I was never really built for that kind of work. I need dirt under my feet."

Mama lets Miss Mavis fold her into a hug. When they let go, Miss Mavis gives me a smile. "I was right about you being brave," she says.

My jaw drops.

"Even if I was good at bluffing," she adds.

"May I hug you, too?" Mama asks Chapel. Chapel nods, and Mama pulls her into her arms. "It's been good getting to know you," she says. "Thank you for being there for my baby."

Even after a night fighting with demons, I'm embarrassed enough about Mama calling me her baby in front of people to grimace.

Miss Mavis looks up at Gevi, and something silent passes between them. He spreads a palm on the ground and Miss Mavis climbs into the valley of his hand. She waves, and he raises her high above the woods and drops her onto his broad shoulder. With a stony salute, Gevi turns toward the woods.

Just then I hear a faint buzzing and look up to see the *S* blinking out of the Slumbering Giant sign again as Gevi walks—no, *lumbers*—back into the depths of the trees.

"You *knew*," I say to Mama. I don't just mean the ghost-mons and Guardians. I mean all of it: Miss Mavis, the evil in the woods, the fact that, apparently, I have magic. "Why didn't you tell me?"

She grabs my hand. "I thought I was protecting you. I couldn't risk losing anyone else."

"I know that you wanted to keep me safe," I tell her. "But I lost Daddy, too. And when you didn't come back, I thought I'd lost *you*."

Mama kneels next to my chair and holds me. "I'm so sorry," she says, pushing a scraggly strand of my hair back out of my eyes. "From now on, I want us both to be honest with each other. Deal?"

I nod.

Then she reaches into her pocket and pulls out some papers. "These are spells Miss Mavis gave me. I want you to have them. It's up to you if you want to learn them."

From my own pocket, I take out the piece of paper with the demon-trapping spell. It fits perfectly into a jagged edge of one of Mama's papers.

"Where did you get that?" Mama asks.

"I found it in your car. So we knew how to set the traps, but without the spell . . ." I realize something. "I thought the missing half showed how to kill them. But it was about setting them free."

Mama nods.

"But the ghosts are gone now," I say.

"*Those* ghosts are," Mama says. "No doubt there will be more. There will always be spirits. And"—she darts her eyes over her shoulder—"other things in these woods. There's a lot of energy here. Not all bad, but not all good, either."

Mama stands and dusts off her jeans as Edwin and Chapel join us. Paul jumps from Chapel's pocket back onto my shoulder, taking a delicate purple thread that's tangled around his back talons. He feels solid there. Real.

A door slams, and Chapel's parents emerge from the motel, calling her name. Before running to them, she turns to me.

"Well, this was an adventure," she says with a huge grin. "There's no one else I'd rather chase demons with."

"Me either," I say, and I mean it.

"We'll hang out again soon?"

"Better believe it." I grin. "I know where you live!"

"Bye, Paul!" she yells, before running off and embracing her parents in a huge hug.

After saying our goodbyes, Mama, Paul, and I set off on a journey of our own, back down the red-dirt road, past the old logging turnoffs to retrieve Mama's car. As we step into the trees, there is a crackle in my headphones, then a voice. *SHE HAS RETURNED.*

We walk for a long time in silence, the three of us just content to be alive and together. "How does the Guardians' radio station work, anyway?" I ask Mama.

"From what I understand, they have a kind of magnetic force," she says. "It has to do with the rock they're made from. It lets them override radio waves to send messages to each other."

"See, what'd I tell ya?" Paul pipes from my shoulder. "Magnets."

Mama looks at Paul, who beams back at her. "I'm sorry I didn't believe you about—about your friend," she says.

"Thanks," I say. "But *I* wasn't even sure I didn't imagine him until last night. No offense, Paul."

"None taken," he says. "I was proud to come from a mind like yours."

There's something about the way he says it that stops me in my tracks. "What do you mean, *was?*"

"Jerry," Paul says in a tone that reminds me of Mama when she's trying to tell me something she knows I know but don't want to hear.

"No," I say.

"All adventures end," he says. "It's time for goodbye."

"It doesn't have to be."

"I came to you when you needed me. But now . . ." He hops from my shoulder to rest on my hand and curls his talons around my finger.

"I'll never forget you," I whisper.

"Course you won't," he says. "I'm not exactly the

forgettable type."

He stands and spreads his wings, and I swear they're just a bit bigger than before. Then, for the second time since I've known him, he lifts off. He hovers above our heads for a second, then he flies upward in a twirling pattern, past the tops of the trees and into the brightening sun.

EPILOGUE

A MOVING TRUCK IDLES IN THE PARKING LOT OF THE SLUMBER-
ing Giant. Its diesel fumes make the blacktop shimmer
above the chalk lines we drew for our own version of hopscotch—one for feet *and* wheels. Curved lines wind around
the squares in rainbow patterns. Chapel's name is chalked
on one side of the court, surrounded by starbursts and
purple butterflies. On the other side, over a drawing of a
dragon with widespread wings and a plume of perfect blue
flame, is mine.

"Is that the last of it?" Chapel calls.

"I think so!" Mr. Bell pops out of their door on the second floor, his arms stacked with boxes. Mama offered to
let them take anything they wanted from the room, but
Chapel only asked for the lighthouse painting.

Mrs. Bell smiles and tucks a loose twist of hair behind
her ear. She slaps the side of the rumbling van. "Let's get
moving, then!"

Chapel's dad slides the last boxes up the ramp and into the cargo bay.

"I'm gonna name a goat after you," Chapel teases.

"No, don't!" I laugh.

"We won't get the goats till we're settled in, but I'm getting a bonded pair of cats! I named them Sam and Dean."

When I look blankly at her, Chapel launches into a long description of some show about two brothers who hunt monsters. I shake my head. I've had enough monster-hunting for now.

"Once we're all moved in, you gotta come visit," she says. "The farm is *so* cool. It's right outside town. We can even come give you a ride if you need!"

I look over at Mrs. Bell, who nods. "Any time, love."

Mr. Bell pulls down the sliding door on the back of the truck, and Chapel swings herself up into the cab. There's a heavy clunk as the engine shifts into gear, and then they're rolling out of the lot and down the hill. I wave until it disappears over the rise.

"Jerry!" Mama calls, creaking open the gate behind me. "Did you forget we've still got moving to do, too?"

"No, Mama." I roll into what used to be our room and scoop up the last of my things, a small stack of books and Daddy's sword, tucked neatly into its velvet-lined case. With a last glance around the room, I pull the door shut behind me and wheel down the walkway to our new apartment, the one that used to be Miss Mavis's.

The runners Mama put on the carpet make it a lot easier to roll through the living room, and I glide to the little storage room that's been converted into a bedroom for me. It's the first room of my own since we left our house. I don't mind the idea of not having a regular house so much anymore. The Giant feels like home now.

Edwin moved into one of the empty motel rooms when he left the logging company and became the handyman here, though he comes over to our place for dinner a few nights every week. I don't think I mind that, either.

I drop my things on my bed and turn around to see Mama leaning in my doorway. "I have a little surprise for you before you put those away," she says.

I follow her to the kitchen table, where there's a small, gift-wrapped box. I pull the ribbon off and open it to find a new cell phone.

"Really?" I lift it carefully out of the box. "It's mine?"

"I think you've earned it," Mama says. "Besides, with you starting school tomorrow, I need you to be able to check in with me."

"Thank you!" I start to slip it into my pocket.

"Wait. I think you've got a number in there already."

I swipe past the screensaver and click on the bubble marked CONTACTS. There's just one number saved so far. Next to the number, there's a circle with a picture of

Chapel's smiling face.

I open the text box and type in my first ever message.
MEET YOU OUTSIDE SCHOOL TOMORROW?

I watch the screen as tiny dots float across, and then Chapel's picture pops up again, next to a message of her own.

I'LL BRING THE CHALK.

Acknowledgments

I'VE LOVED STORIES ABOUT GHOSTS, CRYPTIDS, AND THE supernatural for as long as I can remember—especially the ones where either running *after* those creepy things or *away* from them is an adventure that bonds unlikely friends. But, as a wheelchair user, "running" is not something I can, technically, do. It was while watching one of my favorite paranormal horror shows and finding myself wondering for the millionth time how someone like me would get out of the monstrous predicament the heroes were in that I decided to write that story myself. This, many versions later, is that book.

There are many people this book could not have happened without. My incredible agent, Mandy Hubbard, who has met all of my ideas (even the weird ones) with encouraging enthusiasm, guided and shaped TLGOWP with me and then found it the perfect home ridiculously fast, and has shown me pictures of her cows. My likewise amazing editor, Amy Cloud, who helped me find the heart of the story and get to it, encouraged me to make Windy Pines and the haunted woods even stranger and scarier, and pointed out that I had way too many scenes about vending machines. "Amy wouldn't let you get away with that!" has become a rallying cry in our house whenever we watch something with blatantly handwoven plot holes. Amy made me fix all the stuff I was hoping she wouldn't notice, and this book—and myself as a writer—are better for it.

My family, especially Junebug and Blossom. There are pieces of y'all threaded through all of my characters and all the places I imagine for them to call home. All I ever wished for was to make you proud of me.

My writing circles and creative collectives over the years: Vicious Circle, Raised by Wolves Crew, the Cool Kids Table. The Launch Pad and the people there who literally saved my life. All of the poetry family—thanks to y'all there's not a city I can name in the lower forty-eight where I don't have a couch to crash on. Especially the Southern Fried poets, especially the Atlanta poets, ESPECIALLY Art Amok, my heart. I will always call your mic my home.

The disabled writer squad: Lillie Lainoff, Melissa See, Cara Liebowitz, Sabina Nordqvist, LeQuina Knox. I remember bouncing baby seeds of this idea off of y'all early in the process when I wasn't sure I could actually make anything out of it. Your encouragement, advice, and the inspiration of watching you all grow in your own careers gave me the confidence to take it from spitballing what-ifs to an actual book.

Faith Williams Schesventer, sensitivity reader extraordinaire and a pretty awesome writer herself, who helped me bring Chapel to life with the authenticity I so deeply wanted her to have.

Celia Lowenthal, the amazing cover artist who rendered living-color versions of my characters just how I'd imagined them and understood and captured the way that the woods themselves are a character. I am honored to have your art on my book.

Sidney Everitt, early reader, incredible writer, never afraid to check me, always in my corner. E.M. Anderson, early reader, queen of octogenarian lit, and self-appointed president of Paul's fan club. Lindsay King-Miller and Billie Wood for always being game to talk about creepy stuff. The '24-Ever Slack group. The Disabled Kidlit Writers Facebook group. Everyone at Clarion Books who helped turn this from a manuscript into a real book. All of the writer friends I've connected with through the magic of the internet. All of my fandom geek friends, some of whose faces I've never seen, whose real names I don't even know, but I count y'all as friends anyway.

My little sister Kellee, my first fan, who believed the

terrible book I banged out on my family's hand-me-down Frankensteined computer when we were teenagers was gonna make me a star. Being one in your eyes is enough.

Lyssette, my wife, my best friend, and my biggest love, who never doubted me for a second no matter how much I doubted myself; who loved and supported and inspired me through this whole journey. Your art and your storytelling made my world brighter and made me grow in awe of you. I know you say I could have written this book without you, but it wouldn't have been the same book, it wouldn't have been *now*, and I wouldn't have wanted to.

An honorable mention to my cat, Meg, super-ESA, sweetest loaf in the bakery. I swore I was gonna give her coauthor credit because I pretty much wrote this entire book with her on my lap. She's my own little demon and the ones in the book took shape based on her.

Two of the people I felt guiding me the most while I wrote this book didn't get to see it on this Earth. One is my first teacher, Connie, who crowned me a "writer" at age seven when she picked me to represent our whole school in the regional Young Writers' Conference. I declared it my future career right then and it turns out I wasn't wrong after all. The other is my dad, who I feel echoing through all of these pages. It was his old denim jacket that Jerry inherited from her father, his love of Mel Brooks movies and cheesy Yiddish jokes that gave life to Paul the Fairly

Useless Dragon. The very first "book" I ever wrote—on construction paper with crayon, when I was four, about a giant spider who played basketball—I gave to my dad, and he said it belonged in the library. Look, Daddy. I finally made it.

And finally, thanks to you, Reader. I wanted this story to exist, for the kid I was and for the kids out there now who need to read a book where kids don't get left out of the adventure because they're different. This book is in the world because of you. Thank you for reading.